A MILLION SHADOWS

A LYCANTHROPY FILES NOVELLA

CECILIA DOMINIC

ABOUT A MILLION SHADOWS:

Witches, werewolves, and murder - oh, my!

Former model and heartbreaker Kyra Ellison is accustomed to making trouble, not being on the receiving end. When she's kicked out of her family's Ozarks cabin where she's been taking refuge - okay, hiding - after a wicked ancient syndrome wrecked her old life, she's forced to go to Salem, Massachusetts.

Yes, that Salem, where a murder, witches with secrets, and handsome billionaire make danger irresistible. Kyra finds she's not the only one with secrets and skeletons in her family closet, but some are more deadly than others.

A confrontation with ancient danger and a new foe forces her to choose between the old life she's been craving and the new love that might make everything worth it in the end.

LOOK FOR THESE TITLES BY CECILIA DOMINIC

Urban Fantasy Books:

The Lycanthropy Files
The Mountain's Shadow
Long Shadows
Blood's Shadow
A Million Shadows

The Fae Files
The Shadow Project
Shadows of the Heart
The Shadowed Path

Dream Weavers & Truth Seekers
Truth Seeker
Tangled Dreams
Web of Truth

Steampunk Books:

COPYRIGHT

A Million Shadows

Copyright © 2017 by Cecilia Dominic

ISBN: 978-1-945074-15-8
  Paperback ISBN: 978-1-945074-48-6

First edition: 2016

Edited by Holly Atkinson

Cover art by Melony Paradise of Paradise Cover Designs
  https://paradisecoverdesign.com/

1

———

ENDINGS AND BEGINNINGS

"You need to get out of here, Kyra," Matt said. "And by out of here, I mean out of the state."

I caught the snarl before it escaped my jaw. "You're overstepping your boundaries. The last time we met, you said you couldn't be my therapist, but I certainly needed one."

"And you still do." He looked around the diner to make sure no one eavesdropped. "But being here isn't good for you, either as a person or a wolf. And I'm not saying you did or didn't try to sabotage Lonna Marconi's career, but you haven't exactly managed to prove your innocence."

"I didn't do anything to Lonna Marconi. Why should I even care about her?" I took a deep breath. It had shocked me when Matt accused me of impersonating her to torpedo her cute little social worker career. "As for what's good for me, going to Memphis and trying to re-start my pre-CLS life wasn't."

That had turned into a disaster. Most people thought Chronic Lycanthropy Syndrome was just the hot new behavioral disorder—and for the typical victim, it was "merely" psychological—but a few of us "lucky" ones actually transformed. I figured with enough planning, I could work around my unusual symptom expression. I'd just barricade myself in my apartment on the night of the change, take a Valium, and sleep through it.

I'd wakened that first morning after the full moon from dreams of being trapped, a wrecked apartment, and complaints from the neighbors about being kept awake by the noise of a howling, wild animal. I'm just lucky no one called the cops or broke the door down to rescue me. My landlords were not amused.

Thankfully I hadn't signed a long-term lease and was able to get out of it, come back to the small Ozarks community of Crystal Pines with my literal and figurative tail between my legs —at least on the next night I changed—and try to re-integrate into my pack. But my pack didn't want me, even after I'd apologized for being such a bitch to the new alpha female when I first met her.

Oh, and they'd also figured out my parents weren't dead, like I'd implied when I'd told everyone they'd left me the cabin.

Okay, maybe it hadn't been a great apology, but I'd tried. My pack-mates weren't impressed, especially now that the alpha male and alpha female had started having puppies.

As for the truth about my parents... The pack didn't seem to understand how embarrassed I'd been when I'd first become ill and escaped to Crystal Pines. But that was two strikes against me, hence the meeting I was having now with the beta.

He sat back and shook his head. "Have you thought about doing something different? Starting over in a different part of the country?"

"Running a modeling agency is all I know, and this is my home," I told him. "I just need time to figure this out."

"You've been figuring this out for two years now. You need to find a new pack, start a new life."

I heard what he didn't say—Where no one knows who you are or what a crazy bitch you've been.

He signaled for the check, which he thankfully picked up. Once he paid and I'd sat in sulky silence for a while, he patted my hand.

"I know you don't believe this, but I want what's best for you. You were one of the original Piney Mountain pack members, and you've saved my tail more than a few times. I haven't forgotten that. Please—go and start over. You know the definition of insanity."

I nodded. "Doing the same thing and expecting different results."

"Right. How long are you going to bang your head against this wall? You're letting your condition turn you into a bitter shell of the vivacious young woman you used to be."

He left, and I took a shuddering breath to calm myself. His words chilled me in spite of the warm autumn day.

I was still pondering them when I got into my old Honda, which was yet another reminder of how far I'd fallen as a result of the stupid CLS. I'd had to trade down from the Mercedes I used to drive.

Where could I go? I still had my parents' cabin, which in spite of the rustic name, at least had running water and electricity. But no internet or phone service, and the cell signal sucked up there.

I had four bars in town, though, and just after I pulled out of my parking spot, I was greeted by a ding and a text message from my younger sister-in-law. The blurry black and white ultrasound picture clued me into the contents before I read it.

Welcoming newest Ellison in the spring!

A flurry of dings heralded congratulations from other family members. I drove faster than advisable so I'd have the "no signal" excuse for not replying to my perfect brother's perfect wife's happy news.

The early autumn yellows glowed in the shadowed green forest and seemed to mock my dark, bitter mood. Everyone was moving forward with their lives but me, who was going backward or at least stagnating.

Just before I reached the area where having a telephone conversation would be impossible, my phone rang. A glance at the screen told me it was my mother. As most people with elderly parents do, I pulled over and answered even though I wasn't in the mood to talk to her. My father had a weak heart.

My mother didn't bother with a greeting, just launched into, "Kyra, did you see Lisa's text?"

Instead of answering with an affirmative, I sighed.

"I thought you did. Of all the ways to tell everyone!" Now she exhaled with a huff, and the puff of air coming through the phone irritated me further because it reminded me how similar we were.

"I guess she was efficient."

"She'll figure out how well efficiency works when she has the baby. Nothing throws your life off like having kids."

I stifled another sigh. My mother never missed a chance to let us know just how much she'd given up for us, and I had already anticipated her next question.

She cleared her throat. "Now that the family will have another reason to get together for quiet vacations, I need to know, are you still staying at the cabin?"

"Almost there."

"Look, I've been trying to figure out how to say this, but it's supposed to be a family cabin. Meaning you kids are supposed to take turns, not squat there for years."

I ground the words out one at a time. "I've been sick. I tried to leave, but it didn't work out."

"No more excuses. You have a week. If you need somewhere to land, the house on the Massachusetts coast is free in October. Your father isn't doing well enough to go this year, as much as he loves the Salem festivals. Plus, you'll find more opportunities up there near a big city than in the woods."

That was how my mother did peace offerings—give, take, and offer unsolicited advice—and I knew it was all I was going to get. "Fine."

"Good. I'll send you the information. And, Kyra, we do love you, but you need some tough love. You're driving yourself crazy in those mountains."

I rested my forehead on the steering wheel and tried to focus on it to stop the nauseating sensation of my world dropping out from beneath me. "That seems to be the consensus."

The old Kyra could have handled the northeast with no problem. But now? How long would it be before I broke down completely?

THE WEATHER DIDN'T HELP my mood when I arrived at Logan International Airport in Boston. My nose was stuffed up from the airplane pressure changes, and the low clouds spat a misty rain that I knew would wreck my dark hair into a cloud of frizz even if I pulled it back.

Suddenly my strategy of pretending this trip was a new triumphant beginning—well, allowing my mother to bully me into it in the first place—seemed the dumbest thing I'd ever done. Second dumbest thing. The first, of course, was letting my doctor talk me into the contaminated flu shot that gave me CLS. Okay, this would be the third dumbest thing, the second being pursuing Leo Bowman, who'd dropped me for someone less attractive but smarter.

Well, maybe the fourth...

I was so caught up in my self-recrimination, having documented at least six instances of my stupidity by the time I wheeled my small suitcase outside, that I missed the Salem shuttle by a few seconds. The next one wouldn't be for another hour.

I cursed to myself, particularly since the rain blew sideways in hard wet drops, finding the cracks between and below the departures drive above. Just my luck, the terminal was under construction, so I'd had to walk to where there was a gap in the cover to find the shuttle. I blinked the water from my eyes, not caring if it was tears of frustration or raindrops. So what if I arrived at the coast looking like a frizzy wet rat? It wasn't like I needed to impress anyone.

A large black car swerved to the curb and found a puddle, splashing the gray suede ankle boots I'd indulged in just before leaving Arkansas. Of course I hadn't checked the weather. I cursed, this time not under my breath, at the driver and stepped back to inspect the damage.

Unfortunately I didn't look behind me and bumped into something solid, which I bounced off of, twisted an ankle, and landed straight on my ass, soaking my designer jeans.

No, I wouldn't be making a great impression on anyone soon.

"Why don't you watch—oh, Miss Ellison. What are you doing there?"

I looked up into the hazel eyes of Jared Steel, billionaire and the man who was supposedly the world's most eligible bachelor. At least he had held that title when I'd done business with him, but the lack of a ring on his hand told me he had likely not been snatched up yet. Plus, even in my isolation, I was pretty sure I would have heard something if he had paired off.

He held out a hand and lifted me easily to my feet. His driver picked up my bags and tossed them into the trunk of the car. I kept my purse.

"What do you think you're doing?" I asked. I'd met him on a few occasions in my old life and found him to be as handsome, charming, and sexy as gossip made him out to be.

Jared gestured to me, and his mouth twitched like he tried not to smile. "Well, obviously since I've ruined your boots, soaked your jeans, and knocked you on your ass, I'm going to have to at least buy you dinner to make up for it all."

"Thank you, but no." I walked to the trunk and tried to keep the driver from closing the lid on my stuff. "I was on my way to grab a rental car. I have an important meeting on the coast."

"Then let me take you. It will be more comfortable than driving yourself, and you can get out of your wet clothes."

I arched an eyebrow. "I'm not interested in that kind of ride, Mr. Steel."

His dimples showed when his lips reminded me of how his smile had always threatened my resolve to not mix business with sex. "I meant I'll take you to my condo first, let you change, then take you to the coast. Please let me do it to make up for this harsh welcome to Boston. I can also lend you a car while you're here."

"Going to your condo sounds equally suspicious." But the water was seeping into my underwear, so his offer sounded quite tempting. All I wanted was a hot shower and a good meal. And dry undies, which would be easy to find in my little suitcase. I was thankful I'd carried on, whereas before I was missing my large wardrobe and multi-piece set of matched designer luggage.

"Don't worry, my sister and brother are there. Cindy will make sure nothing happens to you. You can trust me." He gave me that crooked megawatt smile that graced the covers of magazines and the front pages of websites that pretended to be about news.

Jared Steel was known to be a gentleman without even a whiff of scandal around him, but still... He might have good people for damage control.

Meanwhile, an uncomfortable chill, damp sensation was creeping up my ass crack. My mother always said that wet underwear muddles a girl's thinking. I'm pretty sure she wasn't talking about rainwater, but...

"Thank you," I said and tried to seem my old haughty self. "I'll take you up on that offer to grab a quick shower and to change clothes."

2

SHOWERED WITH ATTENTION

Just my luck, Jared wasn't kidding about his brother and sister being at his "condo," a two-story townhouse tucked away in the Back Bay area. His twin brother, Ted, was slightly taller and lankier with lighter hair—brownish rather than blackish—but he had the same hazel eyes and heart-stopping smile, although there was a definite quizzical air to it.

"And who's this?" he asked.

"You remember Kyra Ellison," Jared said. "She runs that modeling agency in the Midwest. We poached some of her girls for reps when you were still with the business."

"Ah, right." Ted had the courtesy to look sheepish. As I recalled, I'd had a few choice words for the brothers when I'd found out, but I was glad for the girls now. Pushing drugs was a much more secure career choice than modeling. Or running an agency.

"Jared, stop gloating. Can't you see the poor girl is freezing?" Their sister Cindy was cute and petite and disgustingly nurturing and positive—everything I hated in other women.

Still, I had to appreciate how she saved me from any more

conversation by bundling me up to the bathroom and settling me with towels before leaving me to shower in the world's nicest bathroom. Fine, I'm exaggerating. The queen of England might have had more real estate where she takes her royal dumps, but this place was impressive with its smooth marble and black and white tile accents. Plus the shower had two, three, no four heads counting a handheld one. After being in the cabin with its ridiculously small water heater, I was in heaven. I could almost forgive Jared's snarky comments.

Whatever. If he was going to save me from a two-hour drive with a wet bottom, he could gloat. Those girls and all the others I'd mentored worked for someone else now, anyway.

Oh, right, he thinks I'm still the old Kyra.

It took me a moment to remember who the old me was. Someone confident and assured. Someone for whom the loss of new suede boots wouldn't mean much, only that I got to go shopping again. Someone who had more than one pair of designer jeans and could afford to throw the old ones away.

I didn't realize I was twisting the soft, thick washcloth into a tight cylinder until I heard something tear. I looked down to see I'd ripped a hole in it. Damn that lycanthrope strength. It sneaked out at inopportune moments—like this—and was a constant reminder of what I'd lost and the act I now had to put on.

I finished my shower, dried my hair, and put on what I hoped was a chic outfit of khaki pants, blouse, and cute jacket. All of them had come from bargain shelves or consignment stores. The boots were likely a loss, but I took them with me anyway. Maybe I could brush out the suede once it dried so it wouldn't look too bad from afar. The only other shoes I had were sandals—definitely weather inappropriate—and my sneakers.

Sneakers it would be. I couldn't pretend forever.

After repacking, I wheeled my suitcase out to the upper

foyer. Before I could lift it to take it down the stairs, Jared came out of the room across the hall from the master bath and said, "Allow me."

"You don't have to do that," I told him.

"It's my privilege."

He hoisted the bag like it weighed nothing, and I followed him down the stairs. He wore jeans now, and I couldn't help but admire his nice ass as he descended in front of me.

"Thank you for letting me freshen up," I said. "You have a lovely place."

"No problem. I'm sorry again for ruining your boots." He set my suitcase by the front door and took out his wallet. "Will three hundred dollars cover them?"

That was what they had cost new, but they'd only been fifty at the Crystal Pines consignment store. I'd watched them until they'd been marked down enough to afford. I couldn't make myself tell him, though.

He misunderstood my hesitation, pulled out three more hundred dollar bills, and handed me six hundred dollars. "Here, this should hopefully cover the shoes and the jeans. Again, I apologize."

As much as I didn't want to, I tried to push the money back at him. "You're being much too generous."

"I remember you're a woman who drives a hard bargain, but can we call ourselves even?" That smile again, but this time with an endearing sheepish element. He wrapped my fingers around the bills. "If it's too much, go have dinner on me. I've messed up your plans enough."

"Thank you," I stammered, and I put the bills in the pocket in my purse where my wallet resided. I'd never had any trouble expressing myself before, especially not to someone with whom I did business. What was wrong with me? And why did I feel guilty for taking money that would allow me to eat while I was there when the pity money my parents had given me ran out?

That was it—I hated for people to feel sorry for me. Joanie had pitied me as she'd stolen Leo from me. Then her snotty friend Lonna had felt the same—I had seen it in her face when we talked. I kept myself from snapping at Jared but asked myself what the old Kyra would do. She'd have a hell of a lot more poise than I did at that moment, and that pissed me off even more. I wanted to shove the money back at him and escape from the memories of what I'd once been.

"You're very welcome," he said. I remembered how six hundred dollars was pocket change for people like him, as it used to be for me. He added, "Are you sure you can't stay? I'd love to catch up, see what you've been doing. It's been what, four years?"

"Positive, and it's been a while." I had to get out of there and away from his smile and charm.

There was something wistful in the way he'd asked me to stay, like he was also missing something from before. Part of me wanted to confide everything to him and turn into a blubbering mess on his broad shoulder. Then he'd really feel sorry for me.

Plus the teasing camaraderie he had with his siblings reminded me of the rift between me and my brothers. We'd never been that close, and then their girlfriends and wives had become the sweet, compliant daughters my parents had always wanted. Now I was the difficult child and the screw-up.

And the outcast. I almost cringed at the sense of the guillotine of time hanging over me—Halloween was my deadline to find something up here and start a new life for myself.

"That's right." He tapped a finger on his upper lip. "You'd become ill and had to sell your agency. I was sorry to hear that."

"Me too." I needed to escape from this conversation.

"But you have business on the coast. That must mean your health has improved." He rubbed his eyes, which struck me as odd. "That's good—if you don't have your health, you don't have anything."

"Are you all right?" I asked.

He shrugged, but his smile had lost some of its wattage. "Just a headache. Nothing to be concerned about, but I'm afraid I can't take you to the coast as I'd planned."

I usually tried not to draw on my lycanthrope senses—no reason to encourage them—but I took a surreptitious sniff. There was something odd under his masculine odor of after-shave, soap, and detergent. Not cancerous or deadly, just odd. Then the congestion, which had cleared in the shower, returned before I could analyze further.

"I hope you figure it out soon," I said and meant it. There was something comforting in knowing the world as I remembered it still existed for some people, even if I was jealous of them. "It's hard to step back and take care of yourself."

He nodded, and his face assumed the charming business mask I knew well. "Well, I don't want to hold you up anymore. I've had a car brought around for you. It's one of my older ones, but it should run well."

Again, that careless wealth produced twin stabs of annoyance and envy in my gut.

"Oh, you don't have to do that. If your man will give me a ride back to the airport, I'll take the shuttle."

"Nonsense. I'm not using it. This way I don't have to pay to park it and it'll save you some money. Take it as a favor to me." He opened the door, and the driver came inside and grabbed my suitcase. I picked up my purse and smaller bag and tried not to resent him for assuming I needed his help.

"I'd really prefer a ride back to the airport since I don't know what my parking situation will be once I get to the house."

"A house? You're moving here?" His eyebrows flagged his interest, and I bit my tongue.

"Thinking about it."

"Ah, a woman of mystery, as always. I'll have Edwin take you to the airport, then."

"I can't take that much advantage of your generosity." I lowered my eyelashes—dear gods, where had that come from? The old Kyra was trying to come out and flirt with him. "I can take the train."

"Let me at least do this for you. And call me."

My brain tried to resist and end the interaction then, but my traitorous tongue tripped out my phone number almost of its own accord.

He programmed my number in his phone and texted me his. "Good. And keep me in mind for dinner sometime. I'm scouting locations outside of the city for a new office, so I'll probably be up your way. If you need anything, text me or call my assistant."

Cindy walked out of the kitchen and looked up, seemingly surprised to see us. "Oh, are you leaving already?"

"I'm afraid I have to. Business awaits," I said. "I should get back to the airport to catch the Salem shuttle."

"Oh, I'll drive. It will be good to catch up."

"Thanks, Cindy." He gave her a kiss on the cheek, pressed a business card into my hand, and escorted me to the waiting Jaguar. He held the passenger side door open as I got in and closed it once I was settled.

The car was already running and was warm, and I ran my fingers over the supple leather seat.

Good lord, I remember luxury like this.

I hoped my smile seemed genuine, and I waved to him as Cindy pulled away.

"It's such a nice surprise to see you again," she said and merged into traffic. "It's been a few years."

"Yes." I didn't really want to talk, so I looked out of the window at the cute boutique shops and fancy restaurants.

Would I ever be able to afford them again?

"Jared talked about you after that one party, but then things got busy with the company, and you disappeared. Some sort of health problem?" Her tone conveyed concern, but I didn't take the invitation.

"Yes, my life took some unexpected turns."

"That's too bad. Well, now that you're here in the state, we'll have to have lunch sometime. Do you know when you might be free?"

"No idea, sorry." I tried to give her a rueful smile but feared it came out as more of a grimace. "Things are still pretty up in the air."

"Oh, no worries. I'll get your number from Jared and be in touch. Oh, there's my favorite stylist—they have the best deals on products the last weekend of the month..." She chattered on about various stores and other places, and I managed to half-pay attention and half-wish for the encounter with her chipper self to be over with.

Arriving at the airport was a relief.

"Thanks for the ride," I said.

"You're very welcome! Have a great trip up to Salem."

When she pulled away, the stuffiness in my nose released with a torrent of mucous, and I had to dig in my pockets for a tissue. I appreciated her treating me the same as she would have before my illness and disgrace, but it highlighted the difference between life then and life now. I kept it together until I got on the Salem shuttle.

But when I hit the highway, I didn't try to stop the tears of grief for my old life. The old Kyra was still in there wanting to emerge—why wouldn't she leave me alone?

～

Once I left the city, the clouds broke up and revealed the kind of blue sky that only happens in autumn. Whereas the leaves in the Ozarks were in their early autumn show, the trees in Massachusetts put on their full autumn pageant with yellows, reds, and oranges. I wished I could enjoy it, but my mind kept playing over the encounter with Jared Steel.

He didn't have to be so kind to me. Was he expecting something in return that he would cash in on later? That was typically how men worked, but I'd thought he was different. Of course as the CEO of a major pharmaceutical company, he would have to have a mind for business. The question was how much of that ruthless *quid pro quo* philosophy he put into his personal relationships.

Oh, right, you don't have a personal relationship with him. You're not part of that world anymore.

He seemed to know how far I had fallen, or he'd researched it while I was in the shower. Right, because he'd mentioned my business in the present tense when he re-introduced me to his brother. Maybe that was why he'd decided against bringing me to Salem himself—I was suddenly not a worthy investment of time since I was no longer in his business league. I thought I was still beautiful, but Matt had called me a bitter shell.

Was that what other people who'd known me before saw— a haggish shadow of what I used to be?

The bright colors of the trees and sky dulled with my mood. The shuttle dropped me off at the nearest hotel to my parents' neighborhood, and I walked to the house. When I opened the front door with the key my mother had mailed to me, the salt smell of the air outside melded into the fresh, pine-scented odor inside.

Memories flooded back, and I closed my eyes to catch them.

We'd spent summers up here as kids, and I remembered my grandmother bustling out of the kitchen with a plate of fresh Italian cookies to meet us when we arrived. She was long dead, as was my grandfather, but my father hadn't been able to let go of the house.

Suddenly, a desire to go into Salem overtook me. It was so strong I felt like I'd been pushed, but when I turned, no one was there. I'd been pining over my old life, but what if I went back to my old old life before my success, back when I was a student and was just starting out with a sense of wonder about everything? Was that even possible?

I made a quick check of the house and I found that someone had come and turned on the water and heat for me—probably the caretaker my parents hired to manage renting out the place and get it ready for their infrequent visits. What had my mother told her? That her failure of a daughter was coming to make a last-ditch effort at putting her life back together?

Whether I was bitter or nostalgic or wondering, I needed to get out of that house.

The walk into downtown Salem took about thirty minutes. As my feet remembered the way, I enjoyed the colonial architecture and the crisp sea breeze, which felt like it blew the cobwebs away from my brain. With it being mid-October in a place famous for its witch trials and a month-long Festival of the Dead, each neighborhood vied to outdo the others with its decorations. Some houses had large fake spider webs with giant spiders in them and others witch dummies over cauldrons filled with dry ice or something that made them smoke. And, of course, plenty of skulls, mostly human, but I looked away from a few that resembled canines.

I didn't need any reminders that my kind would have been burned, hanged, or pressed to death several hundred years previously.

As I got closer to town, more people appeared on the sidewalks and going in and out of stores. Some were already in costume. At least I think they were in costume. I stopped at a coffee shop for a cup of tea and a turkey sandwich.

Once I was sitting by the window and watching the people outside, the nostalgia wore off, and I wondered what I was going to do here. I had very little knowledge of Salem beyond what my vague childhood memories told me, and I didn't know anyone.

Again, there was a sensation like a nudge at the back of my brain telling me to go farther downtown toward the tourist center and the museums. It had been so long since I had any kind of direction that I had to follow the urge, if only to satisfy my curiosity.

I couldn't tell why, but I followed the urge with its mental directions like an internal GPS down streets I'd forgotten about long ago. My feet carried me to an indoor gallery with an arched glass roof over a common area packed with people resting at tables. An assortment of shops, including a crystal and rock boutique store, lined either side. I recalled from my childhood how I loved to go into that sort of shop and look at the shiny, pretty things.

Back when I was a shiny, pretty thing myself.

A bell over the door chimed when I walked in. A woman seated behind a register looked up. Her straight gray hair stood up in several directions like she'd been running her hand through it or grabbing it in agitation. Although not pretty, she had a striking face with a strong nose and the greenest eyes I'd ever seen on a human. Her pale skin set them off, and I felt like the ground shifted when she looked at me.

Yep, time to get out of here.

Before I could turn, she said in a Scottish accent, "Oh, good. You're here."

I looked around. Had someone walked in behind me? No,

we were the only two people in the shop. "I'm sorry. I don't think I'm who you were expecting."

"Of course you are." She hopped down from her stool and came out from behind the counter. She must have been about five feet tall, and I tried not to stare at how quickly she moved in spite of her plump build.

"No, really, I just came in town today. I'm only visiting for a little bit."

She walked around me, her head cocked and her eyes narrowed. As a former model, I'd undergone my share of scrutiny and harsh feedback, but her examination made me more nervous than I could remember feeling, even starting out. My mind tried to guess what she'd find at fault, how I was bloated from the plane trip, my eyes had circles under them from not sleeping and too much frustrated weeping, and my clothing all secondhand.

"Hard on yourself, aren't you?" she asked.

"I didn't say anything." But I still pressed my lips together. Had I spoken my thoughts?

"I can see it in your face and the set of your shoulders. You've had a hard time lately and need a job. The girl who was supposed to start today didn't show."

"I'm not looking for a job. Why would I be?"

She made a clicking noise with her tongue. "Why wouldn't you be? Your aura tells me you're lost and in need of someplace to settle, and living takes money. You can't survive on just your looks."

"My...aura? Sorry, this is getting too weird." And I used to support myself with my appearance.

I turned to go, but she put a hand on my wrist. I froze, like seriously froze. I couldn't move if I wanted to. Comfort and soothing flowed from her into me. The feelings made for an odd mix of fear and settled into something I didn't know I'd been missing. For the first time in weeks, I took a deep, full breath.

"There, now." She released my wrist and patted it. "I'm sorry, I forget that people aren't used to me, not even the locals yet. I'm Veronica Chalice. This is my sister's shop, but I'm minding it for her while she's being treated for cancer." She gestured around her. "And I need help."

"I'm sorry, but I'm not available right now."

She clicked her tongue again. "That's not true. You just don't realize it yet. I put out there that I needed someone to help me who knew about the strange world of magic, and in you came. Tell me, truthfully, you felt drawn here, didn't you?"

I didn't trust my tongue—it wanted to spill the entire story—so I just nodded.

She peered into my face. "And you know that there are more things in this world than most people are aware of, even if you don't accept them for yourself beyond what you have to."

Another nod. *Can she tell what I am?*

"Those who are special like you need help. I can tell you where it's safe to run after you change and where to stay away from, especially now that it's our busiest time of the year and the area crowded."

Oh, dear gods, she's a real witch. And she knows I have CLS and wants to help me.

"And what do you want in return?" I asked.

"No lying. That's the first thing. And I want—no, need—someone like you to work for me. You can sniff out the shoplifters and dishonest people. I also suspect you can tell who needs what stone."

"I'm not a witch," I told her. "Yes, I can sniff out strangeness, but not dishonesty, and I have no magical ability."

Am I really here having this conversation? Part of me felt like I was standing there watching my bewildered self interact with the Scottish witch.

But I can't deny that something drove me here, and I do need some sort of income. That six hundred dollars won't last me too long up here.

"You probably have more than you know. Most people, especially those who are touched like you've been, do." She stepped back and gestured to the store. "Close your eyes and tell me which stone speaks to you."

I closed my eyes, but the door chimed. I opened my eyes to see a young policeman walk in.

"Excuse me, are you the owner of the store?" he asked me in a classic New England accent with no "r's."

I indicated Veronica. "She is."

"Ma'am, I have some questions for you. One of your employees was found dead at her home this morning."

3

WITCHY WANDERINGS

The policeman asked his questions, and Veronica answered as best she could. Unfortunately, she was the only one at the store the night before and that morning, and she hadn't made any sales, although plenty of people had come in to look. Still, as she said to the cop, the tourists all blended together once the season picked up, and she couldn't really give a clear description of anyone. And her sister had gone to bed early.

"That's fine," he said. "I'll ask your fellow shopkeepers. It's too bad your sister can't alibi you."

She narrowed her eyes, but he'd already turned to me. I wondered if he'd transform into a newt later.

"And what's your name?"

"Kyra Ellison."

"Do you work here?"

Veronica gave me a pleading look, and the hard shell I thought I'd wrapped around my heart cracked. Sure, she didn't know me from Eve, but she needed me, as opposed to my own mother, who had sent me as far away as she could.

Plus, Veronica was going to be short-handed, and if she was

going to be a person of interest in a police investigation, she wouldn't have time to mind the store. I'd only known her a short time, but I felt protective of her, although I suspected she didn't need my help in that way.

Seriously, I wondered if the cop was going to turn into some sort of reptile later.

I smiled. "I guess I do now."

"And did you know Crystal LaForge?" he asked.

I almost asked if that was a stripper name, but I tamped down my inner smart ass. "No, I just got in town today." And someone named Crystal was going to work there?

I was no detective, but it seemed a fishy coincidence or at least weird. But then, everything about this situation was odd.

"Can you tell me who can verify that?"

"You can check with the airline." I gave him my flight information and, reluctantly, the number for the caretaker of my parents' house. I had no doubt my mother would be hearing about my tangential involvement in a mysterious death —"We're not calling it a murder yet"—sooner than I'd like her to.

"And is there anyone else who can vouch that you weren't in Salem until this afternoon? Your timing doesn't work out if your flight got in at nine."

"I was visiting a friend in Boston." Uh oh.

"And this friend's name is...?" He paused, pen poised over paper.

I gritted my teeth. "Jared Steel."

His eyes widened, but I couldn't tell whether it was from shock or disbelief. Both pissed me off.

"The billionaire pharmaceutical guy?" he asked.

"That's him." Of course everyone would know who Jared Steel was. He was a legend in the state. My cheeks heated to the color of the magenta stone on the shelf beside me.

He either thinks I'm lying or that I'm showing off.

Veronica only looked amused.

"Great, I'll check with him. His people. Him." He raked his fingers through his hair and snapped his notepad closed.

Veronica and I shared a smile over his head.

After he left, she shook her head and said, "I don't know whether to cry about Crystal or laugh at how you flustered that poor young man."

Poor young man, huh? Guess he won't be transforming into anything slimy later.

She hopped back down from her stool and walked around the counter so she could look me straight in the face and say, "You didn't mention you have a relationship with such a powerful man."

"I don't have a relationship with him. He let me change clothes at his place after I fell into a puddle at the airport."

"And..."

I huffed. "And he offered to let me borrow his car, but it was only a Jaguar." As soon as the words left my mouth, I knew how silly they sounded. "I refused."

"Men don't trust others with their machines lightly," she told me. "I suspect you'll be hearing from him sooner rather than later."

I held my breath, expecting my cell phone to ring, but it didn't. "Later, then."

"Good. Let me show you around the shop and how to work the register. I've worked all day without a break. Oh, and why didn't you tell me your name was Mercy? You can't get much more Salem than that."

Is she senile?

"It's not. It's Kyra."

"Ah, but that's how you got your name, isn't it?"

Now a shiver tickled the back of my neck. My mother had said she and my father couldn't decide what to name me until one of the nurses had walked in on my mother holding me and said, "Lord have mercy, that's a beautiful baby!" They had decided to play on the Latin Kyrie Eleison—Lord, have mercy—since my last name would be Ellison until I married.

"Yes," I squeaked.

"I'm sorry, dear, you'll get used to me. If there's something you don't want me to know, just put it under a blanket in your mind. I can't help being nosy sometimes, especially when I'm under stress." She shook her head. "Poor Crystal. I'd so looked forward to her working here—her name was just perfect—but I was going to fire her for not showing up on her first day. I felt bad enough about that, but now I feel awful." She smacked one small fist into her other hand. "And I should have known something bad would happen to her, but I didn't sense anything."

I wasn't sure if her not knowing her former employee would die made me feel better or worse about her witchy abilities. "Maybe there are some things we aren't meant to know."

She inclined her head. "You're a wise young woman, even if you don't give yourself credit for it. Now, tell me which stone needs to be yours. Then I'll give you the tour, training, and paperwork. Do you have proof of citizenship?"

"I think I'd rather hold off on finding my crystal," I said. "This has all been a bit much, but I'm fine watching the store if you need to go grab lunch or something."

After a quick tour of the inventory and a training of how to use the old-fashioned cash register, she settled me behind the counter with the employment paperwork. She also gave me her cell phone number.

"I'm a modern witch, but sometimes these electronic thingies don't work well around me. That's why I still use the antique register. But text me or call if you have a problem. I'll just be in the cafe down the way."

She left, and I started on the paperwork. Name—easy, although I was still freaked out about how she knew its origin. Address—that was harder. My license still had my Crystal

Pines address on it, and my passport my parents' address since I hadn't kept a regular address until I'd gotten CLS and stopped traveling. Prior to that, I had an apartment but would only sign short-term leases in case something better came along.

I put the address of the Salem house since that was where I would need paychecks mailed. I'd also have to find a branch of the national bank I used.

I hadn't unpacked at the house, and my passport was still in the inner pocket of my purse. When I opened it for the number, old Kyra looked up at me. It was a tiny photo, and they had told me not to smile, so I saw the cold haughtiness I'd cultivated. I couldn't remember why, exactly. Perhaps to push people away and make sure they wouldn't interfere with my plans? I couldn't recall if I'd been lonely. Alone wasn't a problem, and I never lacked for male company, but I didn't have many—any— female friends.

I wondered if Cindy Steel would be amenable to lunch sometime. The thought surprised me, but she had seemed open and friendly.

I shook my head. That would be another tie to this place, and I wasn't sure I was going to stay. Although I was now in a temporary position, presumably through the Halloween season, it felt more permanent than I was comfortable with.

Veronica returned from her late lunch with a cookie for me. No one had come in the store, which I found odd since I'd seen plenty of people outside in the shopping center's gallery—a long hall between the shops with a vaulted ceiling. Occasionally someone would peer through the window, but the bell over the door remained silent.

"Why aren't they coming in?" I asked. The stones were displayed on the shelves in an appealing way, particularly in the two glass windows that faced the gallery. I'd familiarized myself with the pricing, and although I didn't know the area that well, the crystals seemed reasonable. I hadn't found any that needed to come home with me, though.

"Those who need to come in will," she said. "After last night's lookie-loos I decided I didn't want to bother with anyone who wasn't serious."

"How?" But then I remembered the nudges that had brought me here. "Never mind, I don't want to know."

She shook her head and clicked her tongue again. It wasn't so charming this time.

"You struggle with your own magical nature, don't you?" she asked.

"I don't want to talk about it." I glanced at the calendar hanging on the wall, and shivered when I saw how close we were to the full moon—the only time when changing into a wolf wasn't voluntary for those of us with Chronic Lycanthropy Syndrome.

"Most would be happy for the excitement you experience."

"I'm not," I said. "I want predictability and security."

"Then you should probably take that phone call, although all is not as it seems with your young man."

"Who? I don't have a young—" My phone rang, and the screen showed it was Jared Steel.

"Go," she said. "I'll show you how to lock up tomorrow."

I waved goodbye, left the store, and answered the phone. After we exchanged pleasantries like we hadn't just seen each other that morning, he asked, "So what have you been up to in Salem?"

"Nothing much, just business."

He chuckled, and the sound came through the phone like warm, dark chocolate. I had the urge to make him laugh so I could hear it again.

"You're selling yourself short with your nothing much. I just got a call from a detective up there asking about your whereabouts this morning." His charming tone took on a chill. "You're not trying to drag me into a scandal, are you?"

I stiffened and almost tripped over a curb. Old Kyra would never have lost her poise like that, and I had to remind myself not to clench my jaw with frustration.

"No. Gods, Jared. I didn't even think about that. I got questioned by a policeman about a suspicious death, but there's no scandal."

"There's a suspicious death, but no scandal." He laughed, and I relaxed a bit. "I knew when I saw you this morning that you'd still be full of surprises. I'm going to come up and take you to lunch tomorrow. I have to be up there anyway."

"I'm sorry, I have to work," I told him. I didn't know if I did or not, but I suspected I would, especially if Veronica undid whatever she'd done to scare people away.

I expected him to say he'd come and meet me on my lunch break, but there was a long enough pause I wondered if the call had been dropped.

"Are you sure you can't get away?" he asked. "I know a great little place in Marblehead."

"I'll have to ask tomorrow morning."

A couple of passersby gave me strange looks, and I realized I was scowling, so I tried for a more neutral expression. There was definitely something off about this conversation. Why was he so interested in me? Well, besides the fact I'd been naked in his bathroom that morning.

Oh, crap, he didn't have cameras in there, did he? No, now I'm getting paranoid.

"By the way," he said, "did you hear the big news?"

"No, what?"

"Someone leaked the story that an institute in Scotland developed a cure for CLS."

4

A BUMP IN THE NIGHT

Jared's pronouncement stopped me in my tracks. Literally. Someone bumped into me when I halted, and I stepped out of the flow of foot traffic with a murmured apology. It was past dusk, and even more tourists were out and about looking at the Halloween decorations, which were all lit up. None of them realized they had a horror movie creature in their midst.

"What?" I asked. "Say that again, slowly. You're breaking up." Or maybe it was my heart beating so fast it sounded like static in my ear.

"There's a place in Scotland called the ILR. You can guess what the initials stand for. They released a statement today saying they've found a cure for Chronic Lycanthropy Syndrome."

My face felt weird, the muscles moving in unfamiliar ways, and I realized I was smiling. Not the polite smile of the businesswoman or the tired moue of the monster exhausted from a night running about, but a real smile. I wished I had known there was an ILR—Institute for Lycanthropic Reversal—earlier. I would have volunteered.

Then skepticism snapped my lips back into place.

"And you believe them? What sort of proof do they have?"

"I don't know, but if my company could get hold of the formula and patent it in the States, it could be huge."

"Do you know who's in charge?" I had a suspicion, and he confirmed it as well as the other reason he'd called.

"The heads of the institute are Maximilian Fortuna and his wife, Lonna Marconi-Fortuna. She's from your neck of the woods down in Arkansas. I was wondering if you happened to know her, could give me an in."

Now we were playing a game I knew well. Perhaps I should have been disappointed he wasn't calling just to ask me to lunch, but I was glad to slip back into the role of impression manager and charmer.

I carefully stepped back into the moving crowd. No one seemed to notice me. They were too busy oohing and ahhing over the houses.

"Let's discuss this at lunch tomorrow, assuming I can break free." Even if I was essentially invisible, I knew how easily people's attention could be drawn by the merest hint of drama. I didn't want to admit to Jared that Lonna Marconi and I had a brief but dramatic history, or that accusations of sabotage had chased me out of Crystal Pines.

"Text me in the morning. And be careful—I don't like this police investigation. You could be in danger."

"I'm sure I can take care of myself."

With teeth and claws if I have to.

The thought surprised me, especially after the hope and excitement that had welled up with Jared's news. I changed into my wolf form when I had to, and although I could otherwise, I chose not to. Why would I embrace something I hated so much —the thing that had ruined my life?

This was not the time to start finding advantages to it.

I was happy when I could break free of the crowd and head

toward my parents' house. Their neighbors cleared out and rented their houses to tourists, but they didn't decorate. When I opened the front door, I found everything as I had left it, but there was a strange sulfurous odor like someone had lit a match.

My feet crunched on something that looked like sand in the front hall. Had I tracked that in earlier?

I made a circuit of the first floor of the house and didn't see anything else strange. Perhaps the caretaker had come and gone, but why would she have left sand in the front hall or lit a match?

I shrugged, grabbed my suitcase and satchel, and brought them to the master bedroom. My mother expected me to stay in what she called "the girls' room," but I wasn't ten anymore. After the cot in the cabin, I wanted to stretch out in a king-sized bed, not contort myself so my feet wouldn't dangle off a twin mattress.

Dinner was a protein bar I'd brought with me and a bottle of water from the case in the kitchen closet. After a quick shower—not nearly as nice as the one I'd had that morning—I crawled between the clean sheets of the master bed. It was barely eight, but I'd been up since four a.m., and soon I was asleep and dreaming of witches who could wave their wands and cure me of CLS, but my health insurance wouldn't cover their procedure because they hadn't gotten the proper pre-authorization.

A MOONBEAM FOUND its way through the blinds and speared me awake at around three o'clock. I rolled away from it, but my movement was echoed by a thud downstairs. I sat up, all senses alert, and heard a scratching sound like boots scrabbling in sand.

I pulled the T-shirt I'd slept in over my head just before my hands curled into paws. My fingernails turned into claws, and the change came on from my extremities. It felt like I curled inward and folded into shapes no human body should endure. The fur itched as it pushed through pores I hadn't had before, but I couldn't control my paws enough to scratch it.

The final thing to change was my face, and that was the worst sensation, of someone taking my nose and pulling so hard it brought my skull with it.

Then the pain stopped, and a sense of strength, grace, and deadliness unfurled like a flag in my middle and filled me with purpose. To my wolf eyes, the room seemed awash in daylight —not moonlight—and my lips curled.

There was an intruder in my house, and I wanted to tear him or her apart.

No tearing apart, I reminded myself. Not unless I want a visit from that nice policeman later.

I jumped off the bed with as little noise as possible and slunk into the hallway and down the stairs. My fur was the same color as my hair—almost black—so I knew I would blend into the shadows.

Whereas the sulfurous smell had dissipated to my human nose, it was still very strong and present to my wolf nose. But that wasn't what made me stop, all fur on end, when I turned toward the front hall. The sand I had stepped in glowed an opalescent blue, and I saw it was in a circle shape about three feet in diameter. I could see the panes of the front door through the ghostly figure that struggled in the middle of it.

My wolf brain, eminently practical, noted that I couldn't do anything about a ghost because it wasn't solid enough to be afraid of me, so I should just turn around and go back to bed.

But then I heard my name.

My ears perked up, and I moved closer, sticking to the darker patches. Why was the ghost calling my name? Was it a deceased family member visiting for the Festival of the Dead? What was I supposed to do about it?

"Kyra, where are you? I'm trapped. I just want to talk to you."

The ghost pushed against some sort of invisible barrier. When I got close enough to make out its features, I gasped, which came out as a canine huff.

Jared Steel was the ghost trapped in the circle.

"What are you doing here? Are you dead?" I didn't know if he would hear my mental voice, but he spun around.

"Where are you? I can't see you."

"I'm right here. It's nighttime. Why are you here in my parents' house? Are you dead?"

"No, I don't think so. I think I'm dreaming." He looked at his hands and grew more solid. I moved out of the shadows to sit in front of him, and he tried to back up, but he bounced against the back of the circle.

"Kyra, wherever you are, go! There's a wolf."

He looked so bewildered I wasn't sure whether to laugh at him or comfort him. I still didn't know whether he was dead, but I suspected not. If some wolves could spirit-walk, then I supposed some humans could, too.

I did want to know who had made a binding circle in my foyer, but I guessed it wasn't my confused astral projection house guest.

And if he was projecting while he was asleep, I could have some fun. My instincts told me he didn't realize he had this ability and would just write all this off to a strange dream in the morning.

As he came more into view, his attire resolved itself into shorts and a tight-fitting T-shirt that hugged the muscles of his upper arms, shoulders, and chest. Dark hair showed above the rim of the v-neck collar, and I licked my lips at the sight of his lightly fuzzed and nicely shaped legs.

Yes, Jared Steel was quite nice out of his work clothes, and I found myself disappointed that he didn't sleep naked.

"*Are you asleep?*" I asked.

He rubbed his eyes. "I suppose so? But seriously, where are you? This wolf looks like it wants to eat me alive. It won't stop staring at me."

"*I'm right here, but I need you to turn around.*"

"Why?"

"*Just do it.*"

With one last look at me, he complied. I changed back to my human form and blinked the tears from my eyes at the sensation of having my face pushed back into place and my body stretched out. As for the fur, it felt like a rough-bristled brush being shoved through my skin.

I remained on all fours and gave myself a moment to recover. Then I stood on wobbly legs and arranged my long hair to reveal my breasts and private parts enough to be tantalizing but not give the whole story away.

"All right, you can turn around."

5

THE UNWELCOME CHAPERONE

A blast of cold air made me cross my arms over my carefully displayed body, and when Jared turned around, his eyes widened with fear, not with lust.

What the hell...?

I turned to see the very angry ghost of my Italian grandmother standing behind me. She held a rolling pin like a weapon she couldn't decide whether to throw or hit me with. Whereas her hair been completely gray when she died, she looked like I remembered her from my childhood with gray streaks, only a few wrinkles, and black eyes that could impale you with disappointment and make you feel guilty for everything you'd ever done.

Since the last time I'd seen her, I'd done a lot.

"Nona?" I asked. Gods, how I'd missed her. She'd been my father's mother but had been able to keep my own mother in line, at least while we were here. Our visits were a rare but welcome respite from our mother's manipulations.

Nona didn't look so happy to see me, though.

"What are you doing, granddaughter? You know that

canoodling between unmarried couples isn't allowed in this house."

"But, Nona, you've been dead for ten years."

"And you've been acting like a slut for longer." She spat her words, and they stung me like a whip. She continued, "House rules still stand. If you're going to tempt that poor young man's projection, you can do so elsewhere. Either put on some clothes or find another place to stay. If I could tell your mother..." She shook her head in that way of hers that said she was praying to the angels for patience.

I looked over my shoulder at Jared, who had a huge grin on his face. "This dream has taken a very entertaining turn," he said, "even if I would have liked it to go a different way."

I'm pretty sure my backside blushed under his admiring gaze. I know the rest of me burned, but I wasn't sure if it was embarrassment or lust for him. He had a body that Renaissance artists only dreamed of, and I wasn't sure how well he could control his astral projection's appearance—meaning that he might have been giving himself some male enhancement. But if not, holy canoodling! He was definitely interested in what he saw.

A smack on the back of my head made me turn back to face my grandmother's ghost. "Stop sinning with your eyes." She waved her rolling pin at Jared, and he disappeared with one of his chocolate fondue chuckles.

"You. Clothes. Now." She pointed to the back of the hallway, where the stairs were. I moved to go around her, but she stopped me with a hand on my arm. "And, Kyra, be careful. While you have a protector here, there are those who want to do you and your kind harm. They have attracted the attention of spirits who are older and more powerful than I."

"What are my kind, Nona? And who are you talking about?"

"You have Benandanti blood, granddaughter, the good walkers of the Italian hills. That's why you have the full expression of the wolf illness. There are those who believe it's only for those of royal blood, and those who believe it is a curse that should be eradicated." She shook her head. "Now go back to sleep and rest while you can. I sense danger around you, but not details as to who. Trust no one, not even that handsome young man."

"I've missed you, Nona."

"I've never been far away from you, my Kyra." She put a hand on my cheek and disappeared.

Something wet fell on my bare feet, and I realized the drops were tears. I hadn't cried for her in years, not since her funeral. Since then, I had been careful not to show any sign of weakness and had fought hard for what I wanted, whether those around me said I deserved it or not.

It sounded like I wasn't done fighting yet.

I woke the next morning fully dressed and wondering if the strange occurrences had been a dream. Even so, I avoided going downstairs. The previous day had been weird enough, and I just wasn't ready to face the evidence that not only had I possibly been seen by Jared Steel naked—damn that wolf brain —but my ghostly grandmother had warned of further threats.

The thoughts bounced around my head like sugar-fed toddlers. I took my time getting ready but found it difficult to focus. Early mornings after changing were the hardest—Damn, another sign that last night was real—because the animal brain took its time going back to sleep. We all had different hangover effects from changing.

Or maybe I'm just exhausted from traveling and all the weirdness of yesterday. But still, thank gods there's a cure.

What had Nona said—Benandanti blood? Right.

Perhaps my subconscious had been trying to fill in the

reasons for why I'd gotten the kind of CLS I had, the full manifestation of the change. Some people just had symptoms—delusions, strong pack mentality, desire to be outside at night—but very few changed. So few, in fact, that those of us who did tended to flee to remote areas, where we found each other and banded together for support and protection.

Or had, anyway.

Matthew's words echoed in my brain, how there couldn't be two alpha females. How did that bode for me in another pack? Would I be seen as a threat and challenge, or would I be punished for trying to fight for what I thought was mine? It was not like Leo had been unresponsive to my attention before Joanie Fisher had arrived.

I tugged my mind back to the present. I'd been pondering which shirt to wear, but it didn't matter. Okay, I tried to feel like it didn't matter, convince myself that I wasn't interested in the world's most eligible bachelor. But I had dreamed he was as sexy as the guy I'd always cast as the hero when I read romance.

It was only a dream, it was only a dream...

I walked down the stairs and didn't see any sign of last night —no fur, no paw prints... The dawn light shone straight through the glass panes and showed that the foyer floor was clean. Really clean. As if someone had come in and swept it.

Had I imagined the sand? Or had salt been used for a spell to bind any intruders that may appear in the house?

Maybe I was feeling something on the bottom of my shoes. But wouldn't there be something on the floor?

Then I remembered how my grandmother had been meticulous about keeping the front hall clean so nothing would be tracked into the rest of the house. She'd always made us take our shoes off when we came in. Out of habit, I felt guilty about wearing street shoes in the house, but I hadn't found the slipper stash yet. Not that I'd looked.

A crash in the kitchen almost knocked me into a change. I

whirled around and darted out of sight from the back of the house.

For the next few minutes, the only noise was my breathing, and my mind whirled. Should I change? If the events of the night before had been real, I would end up too exhausted to meet Jared for lunch if I changed again.

But if I didn't, what would happen to me? I needed more information.

The only weapon I could find in the coat closet was an umbrella with a wicked-looking tip. That would have to do.

I waited for about ten minutes but didn't hear anything else. Hoping that whoever it was had left through the back door after they'd given themselves away, I crept toward the kitchen. It was still pre-dawn, but CLS gave me excellent night vision, another advantage I didn't want to acknowledge.

When I got to the kitchen, I flicked the light on. The room was empty, the door closed and the deadbolt turned to lock.

What had made the noise? Some sort of creature? It would have to be a big critter to have made the crash.

I walked around the island and found the culprit. My grandmother's wooden rolling pin lay on the floor.

I turned tail and ran like a spooked puppy.

I SNATCHED my jacket out of the front hall closet and locked the front door behind me with shaking fingers. The leather provided some protection against the cold but not against the full-body shiver that tried to make me find a corner and curl up into a little ball. At least the sun was already up, and the sidewalk was striped with shadows.

It was real. Oh, gods, it was real.

I had changed. I had exposed myself to Jared, both my wolf self and my naked self. And I'd seen him almost naked. *Not complaining about that part.* And my grandmother said she'd never been far away and had made sure to let me know her spirit was still in the house.

Was that why my parents spent less and less time there, not my father's health? I imagined Nona's ghost wouldn't make my mother feel welcome.

Thankfully my feet found their own way into town. I said a prayer of gratitude to whoever may be listening that the coffee shop was already open, well-lit, and warm. I didn't stop shivering until I wrapped my hands around a cup of black tea and curled up on a banquette behind a little table. The barista brought the scone he'd heated up for me.

"Is there anything else I can get you?"

A normal life would be nice. I shook my head and told him, "No, thank you."

He gave me the kind of smile that young men have been giving attractive young women for ages, but I could barely manage a small grin back. While running my own business, I'd been able to analyze new data as it came up, anticipate what needed to happen, and determine the steps to take to ensure my agency not only survived but thrived. Now I could barely manage my own life, as simple and narrow as it had become.

I got another tea and scone to go. I figured I'd bring Veronica breakfast. She'd had a tough day the day before and had still treated me with kindness rather than taking her anxiety out on me. I could appreciate that since I'd grown up with the opposite. We were both strangers in a strange place, and she was on a work visa, so her position was tenuous. I'd had to deal with similar situations with young models who had come to the States and gone wild enough to attract the attention of the authorities. I would offer my help where I could, but first I had to butter her up so I could have lunch off.

Was I being like my mother? No, I was repaying kindness with kindness, or at least I thought I was.

When I got to the store, Veronica was already there straightening up displays that hadn't been messed. She had dark circles under her eyes and gratefully accepted the tea and scone.

"Aren't you a gem?" she asked. Her accent was thicker this morning, and I wondered if she hadn't slept well.

"Pun intended?"

She blew across the top of the tea and took a sip. "Nice and strong. Thank you, dear." She cocked her head. "Your aura is different. Something exciting has happened."

Her pronunciation and Jared's announcement from the day before clicked. "Yes, right, you're Scottish. Are you familiar with the Institute for Lycanthropic Reversal?"

Her face paled, and she placed the cup on the counter so hard a few drops splashed out. I scrambled for paper towels, which she used to blot the spill.

"What about the Institute?" she asked.

"Someone leaked a statement yesterday that they've found a cure for CLS."

She nodded, and a thoughtful crease appeared on her forehead. "Ah, a leak? They've been working on it since the summer and were close when I left. That's good news indeed, but not for them."

"What did you think I was going to say? This is a lying-free zone, remember?"

"Right." She took a deep breath. "I'm relieved. They have a lot of enemies, and I was afraid they'd been attacked."

"Who would want to attack them?" I sat on a bench. This was close to what my grandmother's ghost had said the night before.

"There's a group called the Purists who feel that CLS is a gift, and they're opposed to the work the Institute is doing. The head of the Lycanthrope Council defeated the Purist alpha over the summer, but there are those who still feel strongly and could act."

I raised my eyebrows. "How do you know all this? And don't say something witchy. Y'all don't get that kind of detail from spells."

She laughed. "No, dear, I'm from Lycan Village, where my own store is. The alpha comes to me sometimes for help."

"And so the Purists are into keeping CLS uncurable. Who else?"

"The Young Bloods are those who feel as you do, who were born lycanthropes and want the option for reversal because it doesn't go well with their modern lives. They typically drug themselves through their changes, but it has negative effects on their health and lives since they have to put themselves out for twenty-four hours."

I caught my breath with relief and excitement. The world had just cracked open and gotten bigger. There were others who felt as I did, that CLS was more than an inconvenience? "But wouldn't they want the ILR to succeed?"

"Yes, but if the Lycanthrope Council doesn't give them a voice or access to the cure, they could turn dangerous."

"Is there anyone else?"

"No, dear. Well, there's the Wizard Tribunal, but they're the lycanthropes' allies."

"What? There are other magical creatures, er, people?"

Her eyebrows angled in a perplexed expression over the rim of her cup. "All kinds," she said once she'd swallowed. "Why are you asking this?"

"I don't know if I'm crazy, but..." I told her about my grandmother's ghost but left out the details about Jared.

"So you have a ghost in your house who's capable of casting spells?" She pursed her lips. "She must have been very powerful in life. You're lucky she's on your side."

I shivered again. "I think she is. Still, that was embarrassing."

Veronica laughed. "Yes, it sounds like seeing her was a surprise. How did she die?"

"Heart failure. She died in her sleep."

Veronica peered at me over the rim of her cup. "Are you sure her heart killed her?"

"That's what the doctors told us. She was in her eighties and had a history of heart disease, so no one felt the need to do an autopsy."

"Interesting." But she didn't elaborate. "At least she won't be going with you to lunch today."

"No. Wait, you knew about that?"

"Just some simple deduction and a lucky guess. There's a distinct glow of rosy hopeful lust about you."

The heat in my cheeks told me more than my aura, or whatever she was seeing, was tinged rosy.

"Just be careful, dear. I know the enemies in Scotland, but there are different dangers here I haven't yet been able to determine."

Her words reminded me of what my grandmother had told me, but the bell over the shop door chimed, and a family came in before I could ask.

Something subtle shifted in the atmosphere. Hadn't Nona said not to trust anyone? For all I knew, Veronica Chalice might be a spy for the Lycanthrope Council.

The shiver at the base of my skull told me my intuition was on to something.

So much for no lying. Or are lies of omission excepted?

6

———

AN ODD LUNCH DATE

We'd been at the shop for about an hour when Jared texted me the address for lunch and, "I'll take care of the valet parking. I hope you like seafood!"

"As if there's anything else to eat up here," I muttered. I knew that wasn't a fair assessment of the New England dining scene, but that was all my parents had taken us out for.

We could never eat at Italian restaurants because we'd insult my grandmother, who, truth be told, fed us well enough. But there was always one night during the visit when we'd go to the beach for a clambake with some cousins and another when my grandfather would take us all out for seafood. My grandmother had a weakness for fried clams with bellies, the soft part, included.

Veronica smiled at me as she dusted, and I tried to put the clams under a blanket in my mind.

"It's nice you have some good family memories," she said.

I glared from behind the register, where I had been studying a list of the stones we had in stock and their approximate prices. "This whole mind-reading thing is unpleasant."

"I wasn't reading your mind, dear. You were muttering about clams, but you were smiling."

"Oh." My face burned again. "Sorry."

She pointed the feather duster at me. "You don't have to be so defensive. Not everyone is out to get you."

"No, just a fair number of them." I pulled my lip back in from where it tried to pout. I remembered my mother admonishing me, "No one likes a pouter, dear. Disappointment shows your weakness. Don't pout—go after what you want."

The bell over the door jangled, and a teenager walked in. She studied the shelves from under heavily shadowed, half-lidded eyes, and she flipped her straight brown hair forward. It had a carefully placed blonde streak from the crown of her head to just below her chin. Her whole demeanor screamed, *Leave me alone* while her cosmetics and clothing—dark and fashionably torn said *Pay attention to but don't fuck with me.* Her face had good bone structure, though her haircut made it look a little too long, and her skin was remarkably clear for her age.

I took all that in before I could stop myself. I wasn't in the modeling business anymore. Still, I kept an eye on her. Her eyes widened slightly when she spotted a shelf with rose quartz, and she fingered a pink and white heart that seemed about the right size for her hand.

I quietly approached her.

"Can I help you, Miss?" I asked in the same tone I would use to address an adult.

"No, just looking." She put the heart down on the shelf with a clack, but her hand hesitated when she tried to pull it away.

"Is it speaking to you?" I bit my lip and tried not to laugh at myself. Had I really just asked her that?

She gave me a classic teenage, but well-deserved, *Puh-lease* —or whatever they were saying these days—look. "It's a rock. A *pink* rock."

"It's a rose quartz." I recalled what I had been reading about it. "That it's carved into a heart is sort of ironic since it supposedly helps people in their love lives. Maybe it'll give it a little extra oomph for you."

She picked it up again. "It's smooth." Then she added under her breath, "I could use all the help I can get."

I could tell she really wanted it but fought with herself over it. Maybe it would take the rest of the money she'd brought with her on vacation. Maybe she was afraid to hope it would be helpful. Or maybe she just didn't want to admit to like something pink. Whatever it was, I stepped back to allow her to make the decision. She replaced it on the shelf and walked around, seemingly looking at other stones, but her gaze kept returning to it. The set of her shoulders said she'd recently endured some sort of heartbreak.

Get used to it, honey.

She returned to it one more time and picked it up, holding it. "I don't have any money with me. Can you keep it for me for later?"

I knew if people went away to think about buying something, they were less likely to commit, but Veronica nodded.

"We'll keep it safe for you, dear. Will you be back today?"

"Yes." A sharp nod made her hair swing forward. "This afternoon. Thanks."

She left, and Veronica plucked the rock in question from the shelf. "I'll just hold this aside for her."

"Don't bother," I said. "She won't be back."

"No, this one wants to go with her, but she needs to put effort into letting it. Just like you do with some things."

"What do you mean?" What I had come to recognize as my natural defensiveness spread like a metal breastplate over my heart.

"You'll know. Now go to lunch. Sometimes the road to Marblehead gets crowded, so it's best if you catch the early bus."

I left. I was smart enough to know when I was being dismissed, and I wondered what I had done to make Veronica impatient with me. Or maybe it was just the usual stubborn Kyra.

Well, that's who I am, and if she doesn't like it, forget her.

If only I could forget the sense I'd disappointed her like I had my mother.

I DIDN'T FEEL like wallowing in self-pity, so I paid attention to what was around me. As with most cute little New England towns, Marblehead had its combination of modern and quaint and about a dozen Dunkin' Donuts within five square miles. Make that most of New England. Dunkin' was like the Waffle House down south—you could never have too many opportunities for a pecan waffle and hash browns scattered, smothered, and covered.

Great, I don't know if I'm homesick or hungry.

I found the place Jared had recommended, which was right on the water. *Good, space is good.* I had already hunched my shoulders as far as they would go while the bus navigated down the town's narrow streets. I wasn't sure what the driver was thinking—there had to be wider lanes for the large vehicle.

I was early, so I decided to walk around until our reservation time. Of course my family had visited the place, but I wasn't nearly as familiar with it as I was Salem.

I wandered outside and along the docks, admiring the colorful boats in the harbor. A crew of men were working on one, presumably to store it somewhere for the winter. A well-built man in a polo shirt and sports coat stood and watched. The boat's sails were furled like wilted petals, its beauty finished with the season. The man I'd assumed was the foreman turned, and I saw it was Jared.

"You're early," he said with a grin, and he kissed me European-style on each cheek.

"So that's your boat?" I asked. My cheeks heated, and I hoped he assumed the pinkness was from the sun.

"Yes, she's a schooner. I decided to take her up the coast one last time today before the winter, and the lads agreed to crew for me."

"That's nice. Kind of sad that it's the last time."

He cocked his head at me, and his eyes echoed the greenish hue of the water. I turned away, ostensibly to watch the activity on and around the boat, but the intensity of his gaze bothered me. What did he see—a failure or an attractive woman? I dared not ask. I could see why women fawned over him—he had looked at me like he thought I was the most important person in the world.

"It's not so sad," he said. "Winter has its own charms like fireplaces, holiday parties, kisses under the mistletoe…"

My mind added, runs through the snow, the magic of the moon in a sharp, cold winter sky, frost crunching under my claws…

I turned with raised eyebrows. "Is that an invitation?" came out of my mouth before I could stop it, but it was the most instinctual thing to say to make sure I didn't blurt out any of what I'd been thinking.

He laughed, and I added hot chocolate to the charms of winter. "Only if you want it to be," he told me, his voice low.

Yep, I'd share my hot chocolate and flirt with him any day, but I needed to know about this cure for CLS.

"Lunch first."

THE HOSTESS COULDN'T TAKE her eyes off Jared, and every time she turned to see if we followed her, her gaze lingered too long.

I thought it would serve her right if she tripped, but she managed not to.

Whispers eddied behind us through the dining room. She led us to a private room and seated us by a window, and I exhaled the breath I'd been holding when she closed the door. I'd once been comfortable with that kind of attention, but that had been when I'd been successful and at the height of my beauty. It occurred to me that some of the diners might have thought I was Jared's latest conquest, or—considering his reputation—that I was trying to seduce him.

Jared hadn't seemed to notice anything untoward, but then, he was used to being handsome and rich and drawing every woman's eye in the room.

"You're a fan of ceviche, right?" he asked.

"I think so." Right, I needed to think about food, not the yummy man in front of me.

"You're not sure?" His perfectly shaped brows flickered into a momentary frown. "I thought I remembered it was a favorite of yours."

"It's been a while." For lots of things, and he knew my favorites? *I wonder what else he knows I like.* I shoved that little thought back into the naughty drawer it had sprung from. "Since I had ceviche, I mean. I don't eat stuff like that in land-locked states unless I know where it came from." A memory tickled my brain, of a corporate party for which he'd hired some models to attend and charm his colleagues, but I couldn't remember much of it—probably because I had just gotten sick. "But I trust you know where to find the good stuff."

"Yes, this chef does it right. We'll start with that. Do you know what you want?"

I scanned the menu—all manner of New England seafood, particularly lobsters and clams, but fresh fish as well. "It all looks good."

"They have an appetizer here that's one of the best kept secrets along the coast."

"Oh?"

"Yes, they do amazing fried clams with bellies." He lowered his voice even though it was just the two of us. "But don't tell my trainer."

"Your secret is safe with me." When I said the words, tingles spread from the back of my skull to my shoulder blades as if something important had witnessed my silly promise. I took a sip of water to clear the sensation. I've been spending too much time with witches. "Oh, and here's something else that's been safe."

I pulled the envelope with his six hundred dollars from my jacket and slid it across the table. "I appreciate you being willing to replace my things, but it's fine. I've got an income, so I feel silly with your money. I shouldn't have taken it in Boston, but I was flustered."

"Are you sure?" he asked.

"Yes." I put all the conviction I could behind the word.

He picked up the envelope and didn't look inside it, just put it in the inner pocket of his sports coat. "All right. And I've never seen you flustered. You're always very in control."

"I used to be. Times have changed."

A waiter came in to take our drink orders, and Jared ordered a bottle of wine and the appetizers. The wine—a crisp white from Italy called Orvieto—appeared almost immediately. After the opening, tasting, and pouring ritual, the waiter bowed out, and Jared raised a glass.

"To celebrate old friends meeting," he said.

"And the discovery of a cure for CLS," I added and clinked my glass against his.

"Right." He didn't say anything else because the appetizers appeared, but once the server left, Jared told me, "I was excited to hear it. I bet it's been tough for you."

I looked around even though we were supposedly in the room alone. There was nowhere to hide.

How did he know? I'd been careful not to let news of my illness be public knowledge. His statement didn't entirely surprise me, though. There must have been speculation when I'd disappeared from society.

But still, CLS wasn't the first thing that people would think. It was still relatively rare among adults who didn't have it as kids.

"It's been hell," I admitted. "But I have to ask—how did you know?"

"I guessed from your reaction on the phone yesterday. You sounded shocked but relieved."

Oh, right. "I was. Both."

"Plus I'd wondered if that's what happened to you. Was it one of the contaminated flu vaccines?"

I nodded and studied the lemon seed that was floating on an ice cube in my water. "Lucky me."

I thought I'd sensed a current of interest, but now he would finish lunch, politely excuse himself, and never want to talk to me again. Why would he want to hang out with a freak and failure like me? I blinked against the burning at the corners of my eyes. Who was I to think I could do this?

The old Kyra would have brazened through lunch, put on a confident face, drunk the wine, and taken what she could. I didn't think I could keep up the act. I was about to excuse myself when he checked his watch.

Yep, here we go, prelude to the polite brush-off. Lunch was nice while it lasted.

"I looked at the phases of the moon online," he said. "Full moon is tomorrow night. Will you be all right?"

I raised my eyebrows. "I suppose."

"Do you need someone with you?"

"I don't think so." Veronica had offered to let me know where it would be safe to run.

Why was he so interested? I took a sip of wine and focused on the burn on my tongue to calm my panic. What if he was the freak? Was he going to proposition me for some full moon sex with my inner animal? Most CLS sufferers only acted like wolves during the full moon.

Boy, would he be surprised if he knew the truth.

The waiter came and paused at the door as if he sensed he was entering at an awkward moment.

"Are you ready to order lunch?" he asked.

"Not at the moment," Jared said. The waiter bowed out.

I took a deep breath. "Look, if this makes you uncomfortable, we can just call it a day. It's not like it would be the first date that's ended because someone found out something about me they didn't like."

"So this is a date," he said. He looked at me over his wine glass, and his lips curled into a smile.

"A business date," I amended.

He leaned forward. "What if I told you that getting the inside scoop on Max and Lonna Fortuna isn't the only reason I asked you to join me?"

Now we were back to the freaky-in-bed hypothesis, but I wanted to make him say it so he would be as embarrassed as I felt.

"What else do you need to know?" I asked.

He looked away, and his throat moved as he swallowed. Yep, he was embarrassed.

"I remember you as a straight shooter and as someone who is very discreet."

And here we go...

He looked at me, and I noticed the dark blue rim around his irises. "I'm afraid I've developed something like Chronic Lycanthropy Syndrome, but worse."

7

PRE-REVELATIONS

Of course Jared's revelation occurred just before the waiter peeked back in. We gave him our orders so he'd leave us alone for a while. After topping off our wine, he disappeared.

The irony of a pharmaceutical drug company CEO coming down with some sort of mysterious ailment wasn't lost on me, but I had no reason to be a bitch right now. He trusted me enough to reveal something sensitive—and, boy, did I know how worrisome this sort of thing could be. But he had a host of underlings to help cover up whatever was wrong with him. I had been running my agency on my own with just an admin, and even she had disappeared once my illness became full-blown and my brain took longer to recover from the changes.

Then I had been a bitch in every sense of the word.

"What's wrong?" I asked.

He took a big swig of wine. "I haven't told anyone." He shook his head. "That is, it's not normal for the Steel siblings to all be in the same place unless my parents are having some sort of event they demand our presence for. They know something is up. Somehow we can all feel it when one of us is in trouble."

I tamped down my jealousy. My siblings couldn't care less if I was in trouble. In fact, it was their fault I was here and not tucked away in the Ozark Mountains. Jared's loss of composure also fascinated me.

"I don't know your siblings that well, but I did think it was odd they were all visiting. Doesn't your brother live in Atlanta?"

"Yes, and Cindy is based up in Portland. I was glad for this lunch so I could get away from them for a while. And see you, of course."

"Charmer." I knew he was prevaricating, but I wanted to let him spill his secret on his own time. I suspected he was having second thoughts about telling me, but I wasn't going to push. We both had secrets we didn't want the world to know.

"I was always attracted to you." He gently took my hand and rubbed his thumb over my knuckles. "The timing just never worked out for me to ask you out. And then you disappeared."

A new wave of bitterness welled up from that broken place in my chest that still grieved what I'd lost. Here was yet one more thing I'd missed out on. Not that I'd been the type to need a man to define me. My independence had always drawn them in. But I'd been attracted to him, too.

"I never knew," I said.

"Bumping into you at the airport was a stroke of luck." He grinned. "Even if it wasn't quite as pleasant for you."

I shrugged, but before I could come up with a witty reply, our lunches came, a lobster roll for me and a cod dish for Jared. They arrived more quickly than I'd anticipated, and Jared seemed surprised, too. He released my hand so the waiter could set down the plates. I suspected the rumor of our pairing off would hit the gossip websites even before we left the restaurant and wondered how much the waiter was getting paid on the side to spy. Or maybe he was just a courteous guy doing his job.

In my experience, it never hurt to be suspicious.

We assured the staff we didn't need anything else for the

moment, and they let us be. Jared stood and locked the door.

"I don't want anyone else overhearing this."

"Are you sure the room isn't bugged?" I asked and then regretted my words when he looked around with a frown.

"Good point."

I couldn't accuse him of being paranoid considering I was just suspecting the waiter of being a spy for the gossip industry. He took his phone from his jacket and turned on an app that sounded like white noise with a high-pitched whine in the background.

A throbbing pain immediately started at the base of my skull.

"It's got a frequency that's too high for humans to hear but will create interference with any listening devices," he explained.

I nodded and reminded myself not to clench my jaw. He didn't need to know that the closer I got to the full moon, the more canine my senses became.

"Are you okay?" he asked.

I tried to speak, but couldn't. He shut off the app.

"Some people have sensitive hearing. We'll talk about this after lunch. I'm sorry." But the look he gave me was one I was familiar with—slanted with suspicion.

"Thanks," I said and gulped some of my water. The throbbing subsided to a dull ache that I hoped would disappear quickly.

Jared kept the conversation light as we ate, but he didn't have much appetite. Unlike me. I found myself happy that we didn't live in an era when women had to keep up the appearance of being delicate and starve themselves to be acceptable to the opposite gender...

Oh, wait. Yes, we did. I didn't care. My wolf was hungry.

The metabolism CLS gave me would have been the envy of any of my former clients—or my former self—and the restaurant did make very good fried clams with bellies and lobster rolls.

I pushed away the thought that with my former career I had helped perpetuate unrealistic ideals for women. But maybe I didn't eat as many of the fries after I remembered how I used to watch everything I ate. Plus Jared nearly made me do a spit-take with the wine.

He was asking me about my grandparents' house and what I remembered of it when he said, "I had the strangest dream last night."

"Oh?" He must be killing time if he's talking about dreams.

"Yes, I was in a house like you described, but I was trapped in one spot, and then a wolf came down the hall."

I put my wineglass down. I'd seen and experienced too much weird crap to discount this as an odd coincidence, and I had originally thought he was astrally projecting. "And then what happened?"

"Well, it turned out that the wolf was you." His cheeks colored further beneath the tan he'd picked up sailing up that morning, but he didn't say anything about me being naked.

My own face grew hot. "That's interesting. You must have been thinking about my CLS."

"And other things." He cleared his throat. "Speaking of which, tell me about what brings you up this way. You said you had work?"

"In a sense. Mostly I'm up here to check on the grandparents' house."

"A new project?"

Reluctant to lie but not ready to reveal the whole truth, I just shrugged and tried to remember what it felt like to look mysterious and evasive. I was afraid I came across as consti-pated, but he nodded.

"Don't worry," he said. "We can talk about it later."

I hoped he would forget.

ONCE WE LEFT THE RESTAURANT, Jared was all business. I wondered if I should have taken advantage of the moment and pushed for him to reveal his secret. I also wondered if I should tell him that I suspected his dream the night before was more like a chaperoned visit.

He put his sunglasses on, and I did as well. The lenses, which had formerly hidden the golden ring around my eyes from the world, now seemed an extra barrier between us. Although he had remained polite, his manner had chilled, and I wished I hadn't accepted his offer of a ride back to Salem from him.

"Tell me about Lonna Marconi-Fortuna," he said as we walked toward the parking garage where he kept a car in a rented space.

I shrugged. "I wish I could help you, but I only met her a couple of times and don't know her at all." Which was true. I didn't mention that one of those times I'd chased her and her friend through a junkyard because I was just off a full-moon change, my brain hadn't shifted out of animal mode yet, and I was pissed that her friend had stolen my boyfriend. The guy I'd wanted to be my boyfriend. Because at the time he had been the best option and I had been lonely and confused, not because I'd actually cared for him.

And I realized it was true—I hadn't loved Leo Bowman. The question was, had I ever loved any guy?

Damn, fried clams make me philosophical.

"You look like you just had a long train of thoughts," Jared said. "I'm sorry. I know you had contact with Ms. Marconi-Fortuna during a tough time for you."

"You could say that." Mindful of the possibility of disappointment, I didn't want to ask what I really wanted to know— did he plan to license the CLS cure to manufacture it in the

States? The thought gave me an unfamiliar warm sensation—hope—followed by a too-familiar bitter feeling—expectation of being let down.

We arrived at the car—another Jaguar, this one a sporty convertible—and he unlocked it and held the door open for me. He waited until we had left and were on the road before he said, "Are you going to tell me what's really going on?"

I turned to him. "Are you? I'm still waiting for you to tell me what's wrong with you. Do you have cancer?"

His lips assumed a tight line, which made a dimple stand out in his right cheek. "No, although at least there's treatment for cancer."

"Do you have CLS? No, wait—you said what you had was worse."

"I'm not sure what I have, only that I know it's serious because otherwise my brother and sister wouldn't have shown up here."

It seemed odd to me that he found no strangeness in his siblings showing up to indicate he was very ill, but I didn't say anything. I didn't know what a close family did, so maybe it wasn't that weird.

"What are the symptoms?"

"I..." He shook his head. "I can't explain it. I have to show you."

I found myself hugging the passenger door of the car. Not that I didn't want to see his, er, assets, but this wasn't exactly the romantic lead-up I'd hoped for.

"Nothing like that, Kyra." He grinned, and both his dimples showed. "I keep forgetting that we've only just reconnected."

I wish I could. I wanted to take his hand, but he needed it for the standard transmission. He'd reminded me of a party we'd both attended when we ended up chatting for about ten minutes before either he or I got pulled away. During that time, it had felt like we were the only two people in the room. I'd allowed myself a few moments of mushiness after, but he hadn't called, and I had dismissed the feeling as me being overly hopeful he'd been interested in me because I had liked him. Like a teenager in Veronica's shop asking her friend on her phone, "Do you like him, or do you *like* him?"

I had *liked* him.

"Why didn't you ask me out before?" I blurted, nothing like the subtle approach I'd thought about. "You said the timing was never right, but what does that mean?"

"Would you believe I was intimidated by you?"

I snorted. "You, the country's most eligible bachelor, intimidated? No, I don't believe that for a second."

"Then you'll have to accept my explanation about timing. One of us was always traveling, or I had a big project coming up, or you had disappeared."

"That's not fair." I stuck my tongue out, and he flashed his right dimple in response. "Speaking of projects, are you going to try to cooperate with ILR to manufacture the CLS cure here?"

"I've been trying to get hold of them, but I can't get past their administrative staff, even when I call myself." His brows touched the tops of his aviator sunglasses frames in a frown. "They're very polite and Scottish, but—" he attempted a Scottish burr "—Ms. Marconi-Fortuna and Dr. Fortuna aren't available to speak to anyone right now."

"That was a horrible accent imitation," I told him, but I might have giggled at his try. "Maybe they're not ready to wheel and deal yet."

"Even if it was a leak, it means they're getting close."

"No, scientists like to show off. Or maybe they wanted to take credit for discovering it first because someone else is about to."

He smiled. "That's more like it. The pharmaceutical industry is cutthroat, and we like nothing better than to be the first. Consider the power Ambien still has even now that it has a lot of competitors."

I suppressed a huff. It felt like he'd been testing me, and I finally made a worthy answer, but why did he care what I thought? To see if I was smart enough to handle his secrets? And why did it matter to me whether he thought I was intelligent? It was not like we had any plans beyond the afternoon, although if he were to actually share his secret rather than teasing me with it...

We turned into my grandmother's neighborhood, and I directed him to the house. He opened the car door for me, and I led him inside.

"Well, this is it, my grandmother's house," I said. I turned to see him looking around the front hall. He hadn't taken his sunglasses off, but his eyebrows arched above the frames, and his jaw muscles stood in tense relief.

"Are you okay?" I asked. I reminded myself to breathe. Here it was. If he was remembering his "dream," then I would have to accept more possibility than I was ready for.

"I... I don't know. This place looks really familiar. I dreamed about it last night." He lowered his sunglasses and looked at me with smoldering eyes. "And you. First you were a wolf, and then you were naked, and..." He rubbed his temples. "This is the sort of thing I was talking about, the strangeness I can't explain."

"Come into the kitchen." I calmed my voice, but a tremble still came through. I'd wanted the events of the previous night to be a dream, and my cheeks flamed at the thought of how I'd acted the horny fool even though my wolf brain had still been mostly in control at the time.

It seemed we had a lot to sort out, and to make things worse, the rolling pin crashed to the floor in the kitchen again.

"We can talk about all this," I said, "But first, would you mind taking your shoes off?"

8

REVELATIONS

"What was that noise?" Jared asked. His sunglasses had disappeared into his leather jacket pocket, and he leaned over to remove his expensive-looking loafers.

The clams with bellies had been lovely going down, but now I tasted the acid and fat at the back of my throat. How much did he really need to know about me and my family craziness?

"It was my grandmother's rolling pin. She was reminding me to take shoes off."

"Couldn't she just come out and tell you?"

"Not exactly." I tried to smile and not look crazy. "She's a ghost."

He grinned like I was making a joke. "Right. This is Festival of the Dead time, after all. And you do have CLS."

It reminded me he didn't know about the full manifestation of the symptoms except—oh, gods—if he realized his dream hadn't been a dream. At least I'd had him turn around for my change. I needed to get him out of there, but he moved past me.

"I'm going to check it out, make sure there's nothing wrong."

"Thanks, but it's fine, really. Maybe you should go."

He whirled around, and I bumped into his broad chest. He steadied me with his arms around me, and I had to tilt my face up to him.

"I'm not leaving until I know you're safe." Now both dimples showed, and I might have melted against him.

"And my dreaming about this place means something," he continued. "You might be able to help me."

"I'm happy to help however you need me to." I hoped he couldn't feel my heart sprinting against his. And that he didn't take my reply as an invitation. But maybe it was. I recalled the chemistry from that party, and the memory of his subsequent coldness made me pull away.

"Right." He turned too quickly for me to catch more than a glimpse of disappointment on his face. Or had I imagined it? My thoughts wobbled between witches, ghosts, and whatever was wrong with him that might have something to do with me.

"Was this the rolling pin you were talking about?" He pointed to where it rested in its little wooden cradle on the island.

"Yes." My hair follicles woke, and everything stood on end at the sense that there was something horribly wrong. If I hadn't heard the rolling pin, what was it? I glanced at the back door and saw it was unlocked and unbolted.

"Or maybe it was something else." I moved to the door. "Someone was here." I flared my nostrils, wanting to sniff out the intruder, but my nose, in spite of being more sensitive than the average person's even when I was in human form, could only catch so much—a clean, floral scent.

So it had been a woman. But what had she done? There was a strange sense of echo—that was the only way I could explain it—in the room, like it stood slightly outside the parameters of reality.

Jared rubbed his forearms through his sleeves, and I tried to not stare. He felt it too? But how? I looked at the door again, which stood locked and bolted, and I gasped.

"What?" Jared asked. He rubbed his temples.

How is this possible? I walked to the door and touched a fingertip to the deadbolt. It was cold to the touch, and I drew my hand back.

"Headache?" I asked.

"No, just a strange sense of pressure. Like a sinus headache about to start." He looked up and dropped his hand to his side. "It's better now. Wait, didn't you say the door was unlocked?"

"I thought it was. Did you see it?"

"Yes." He frowned and came to stand beside me. "I saw the chain swinging, and..." He touched it, then pulled his finger back. "It's blazing. Don't." He caught my hand and showed me his finger, which blistered. I pulled him to the sink, started the cold water, and stuck his finger under it.

"Nona used to have aloe in here," I said. "I wish she still did."

"The water's working. My finger's not stinging anymore."

"Good."

Thoughts darted through my mind and lit up briefly like fireflies, too brief for me to latch on to any one of them. He'd sensed something strange. The lock affected him differently. And somehow he had managed to visit the house the night before through a dream.

The last reminded me of something Charles Landover, a wise old lycanthrope in Arkansas had discovered, how some of us could, with the use of aconite, spirit-walk. I'd later looked up the concept online. The best term I could find was astral projection.

So did that mean Jared was one of us? I would have been able to smell it if he was.

"Tell me about your weird symptoms," I said.

"Now?" He drew his finger from the stream of water, turned off the flow, and dried his hand on a dish towel. "There's too much other stuff happening."

"Every time something odd has happened in this house since I got here, you were somehow involved," I told him.

"Wait, what do you mean?"

I shook my head. "No, sir. You are not going to deflect my question this time. You took me to lunch—thanks, by the way —to ask me about this. You know my secrets." Well, most of them. "It's time to tell me what's going on." I crossed my arms and leaned back against the island.

"Are you sure we should stay here?"

I would have laughed at seeing the world's most assured man so uncertain. "Yes. Whatever it was, it's gone."

"Good. Where are the glasses?" He opened the cabinet nearest him.

"Why? Are you trying to put this off with the old 'I need a glass of water' trick? Small children have been using that as an avoidance tactic for centuries."

"No, to show you. Ah, here we are." He pulled out one of the juice glasses Nona would sip jug wine from. It seemed small and fragile in his large hands, and I remembered how Nona wasn't physically intimidating, but she kept the people around her in line.

As if I needed another lesson in how appearances could be deceiving.

I watched as he filled the glass halfway with water and set it on the island.

"What now?" I asked.

"Just watch." He picked up the glass and cradled it in one

hand. The water inside first clouded, then swirled, and finally bubbled.

"What are you doing?" I couldn't look away.

"I'm thinking of the weather outside, what I'd like it to do."

I looked up at him. His eyes had taken on a particularly green hue. The sense of echo returned, but only around him. *Is that what it feels like to be around magic?*

"So what are you thinking of to make it bubble?"

He grinned at me. "Being with you in a hot tub under the stars on a chilly night."

"That's not weather." But my cheeks heated under his smoldering gaze. Dear gods, I wanted that desire of his to come true. I grabbed a glass from the cabinet and poured some water for myself from the pitcher in the fridge. The sand from outside must have gotten into it in spite of my attempts at rinsing it because something crunched between my back teeth.

He placed the glass on the island and leaned on his hands. "And now the headache."

"You didn't have to hurt yourself," I said and swallowed the grit.

"I had to show you. I couldn't do it at the restaurant in case the waiter walked in or there was a camera in the room. And that's only the smallest of the strange things I've found I can do."

While part of me wanted to drag Jared upstairs and help part of his fantasy come true, he was obviously hurting, and there was only one person I could think of who could help him.

"Luckily I know someone who can help," I said. "She's a witch."

"Really, here in Salem?"

My first thought was that he couldn't be hurting that much if he was snarky, but that was also his MO—to deflect people seeing his true weakness with a joke.

"Yes." I whacked him on the arm. "She's a real witch, not one of the poseurs."

He straightened. His eyes had returned to their normal hazel color—dammit—and I stood beside him, ready to support him. This close, I could see the dark tinge to the delicate skin under his eyes. That little demo had taken a lot out of him. Or maybe it hadn't been the first spell he'd done that day. It had started out cloudy and cool, but by the time I met him, the clouds had seemed to magically disappear.

Nah, I'm just making things up.

Before we walked into the front hall, I gave the rolling pin one last look. Someone had been in here, but I didn't know why. I didn't smell them in the hall, so I guessed the kitchen had been the only place visited. But again, why? Unless someone had a fascination with a ridiculously large collection of Italian juice glasses and hand-crank pasta machine attachments, I couldn't think of what they'd want to steal in the kitchen.

It was more likely we'd surprised whoever it was.

I couldn't justify calling the police, though, since the door had locked itself behind the intruder, so there was no sign someone had been there. Or the intruder had locked it. But how could someone lock a chain bolt behind them?

None of this made sense. Well, it did, but only in a magical way, and my mind pulled back from magic as an explanation in spite of what Jared had just shown me. Sure, I was a werewolf, but my lycanthropy was a genetic disorder from a tainted vaccine.

But what did that make Jared?

He held the door open for me, but the tightness at the corners of his lips told me he still wasn't feeling well. I couldn't help but draw the contrast between then and when I'd found him on the dock. Then he'd seemed full of the life and sunshine around him.

We opted to walk into town since parking in October was especially tricky. He didn't say much until we'd passed a few houses and joined the throng of tourists on the sidewalk. Then he took my hand, and I let him. The contact felt safe, his hand a warm spot in the autumn chill.

"I haven't forgotten that dream I had about you," he murmured.

I could have denied any knowledge of the dream, but my traitorous skin heated in what I knew was a blush.

"And what was that?"

"That you were a wolf who turned into a beautiful woman in a scandalous state of undress. They would have had some things to say about you back in the day."

"They do in this day, too," I couldn't help but flirt back.

"Too bad your grandmother interrupted us. By the way, I saw her picture in the hallway. She looked exactly like she did in the dream."

I tried to pull my hand away, but he held tight.

"You're not telling me everything, Kyra, and I've been completely honest with you."

When I looked up at him, I expected to see anger, not the hurt that turned his eyes dull. The crowd moved us along toward town, and when he released my hand, I had to struggle to keep up with him. It felt like his letting go created a cloud of cold around me, not just the loss of warmth from his hand.

"Some secrets are more dangerous than others," I told him and rubbed my arms through my jacket.

When we reached the gallery where Veronica's shop was, the crowds thinned out, most of the people staying outside and hitting the tourist attractions like the witch museums and the statue of Elizabeth Montgomery in Lappin Park. The tables by the coffee shop were full, though, and Veronica's shop had more than a few people in it.

"Thank goddess you're here," she said when she saw me,

and then, "oh, I didn't know you were bringing some extra help."

Jared looked confused for a moment, then smiled. "I'm just a visitor, ma'am."

"Then I hope you won't mind if I borrow Kyra for a moment." She turned to the older woman who held a stone in each hand. "That's it, just close your eyes and feel which one is friendlier to you."

I took the register and rang people up while Veronica helped others and Jared wandered around the store. Finally we hit a lull, and Veronica locked the door and turned the sign to "Will Return—Joyriding on My Broomstick."

"Thank you," she said. "I should have known it would be busy this afternoon with the nice day." She turned her attention to Jared and studied him with pursed lips. "And what have we here?"

"He's—" I tried to say, but she held her hand up.

"No, no, that's not possible," she murmured and walked around him. "The last one died over a century ago."

"Uh, the last what?" he asked. He shot me a look that was half-panic, half-pleading, but I also thought I caught an amused glint to his eyes.

"You can consider me a crazy old woman, young man, but that won't stop me from seeing what's right in front of me."

Now his face flushed.

"I should have warned you, she can read minds," I said. I shouldn't have been as amused as I was by his discomfort, but it was nice to see someone else on the hot seat. "So what is he?"

She clasped her hands. "Oh, he's very special. He's a weather wizard."

"A what?" he and I both asked.

"A weather wizard. Someone who can manipulate water, air, and energy. One of the most powerful kinds of wizards there is."

9

MORE REVELATIONS

Jared looked at Veronica with the expression one would reserve for a wild animal that had one cornered but that he didn't want to spook. He especially drew back when she asked, "Tell me, have you heard of the Wizard Tribunal? Because they're going to be sending someone to talk to you very soon."

"I'm not a wizard," he said. "I've learned an interesting trick or two, that's it."

"From where?" Veronica waved her hands. "Your power was subconscious for the first three decades of your life. Why do you think it's emerging now?"

He backed toward the door. "Look, I'm not sure what you think I am, but I'm not magical."

"Has anyone given you a book?" Veronica pressed. "Something with spells in it? Or old recipes that don't look quite right?"

"I don't know what you mean." But there was a flicker of something in his eyes.

I emerged from behind the counter to stand beside him. "Veronica, stop. He's overwhelmed."

She narrowed her eyes, which had taken on the color of a cold, cloudy winter sky. "He's lying."

He stiffened, but he didn't refute her accusation.

"Young man, you need to come clean with me. The Wizard Tribunal will not be so gentle when they find a rogue weather wizard has been running around wreaking havoc."

"I've done no such thing," he said.

"Are you sure? It was supposed to rain today. There was a ninety-percent chance." She gestured out of the store to the gallery, where sun poured through the glass ceiling. "What happened to it?"

"Weather changes, especially this time of year," he said. "I wouldn't change the weather even if I knew how. That could be dangerous."

"And it gives him a headache," I added.

"But only if he does it inside, I would guess," she murmured. "What happened to your headache when you walked outside?" she asked him.

"It went away. Fresh air has always helped me feel better. You two are playing a joke on me, aren't you? Trying to scare me because it's close to Halloween." He looked at me, then her. "I know a trick with water, and I get headaches, but I'm not some all-powerful wizard. This isn't Harry Potter. I thought you were going to bring me to someone who could help me, Kyra."

His disappointment pricked me, and I quickly said, "I thought I was, too. Veronica, can't you do something?"

"He's under the jurisdiction of the wizards. I can help him to learn to manage his power, but I dare not do too much because they'll want him properly trained. I'm sure they'll be here soon." But she didn't sound sure or reassuring.

He turned to me. "Do you believe all this? About wizards and tribunals and powerful magic?" His grin faltered, and his expression begged me to say no.

"What if I told you I did?" I held my hands palm-up. "And

you've seen it. You came into my grandmother's house last night."

"Astral projection, or spirit-walking, is one ability wizards have," Veronica told him.

"That was only a dream." But I could tell he didn't believe the words he said, particularly since he'd seen the pictures of my grandmother and recognized the house.

I knew how he felt. The realization of what my first change had meant had hit me with the same force. Once the knowledge that you're a strange, magical creature doomed to forever be outside the bounds of human society explodes in your brain, it can't be unknown. I'd found that denial is the first reaction, the mind's attempt to cushion the blow, but it's dangerous. If I had accepted and adjusted sooner, I might not have lost everything to my CLS.

And that realization hit me full-force, peeling back another layer of denial. At least I was a different person now. It was too late for me to have the life I missed, but I could still help him.

"It wasn't a dream." I held his hand. "You were there, and you were trapped in a circle of binding her ghost somehow made."

"But there was a wolf." He jerked his hand away. "You were the wolf. But how is that possible? CLS is a neurological disorder."

"You need to show him," Veronica said.

My blood thrummed as the CLS genes activated, and the million shadows gathered and spread. I could feel the moon in her fullness peeking from the other side of the world, calling to me to change and howl.

"It's not private enough here," I said through clenched teeth. I closed my eyes and willed the change not to happen, not here in front of him, and especially not in a place with huge glass windows where anyone could see.

"Kyra, what's wrong?" Jared asked.

"I don't know if I can stop it," I told him. When I opened my eyes, the shop looked different, and the shifting between wolf and human vision, back and forth, made me dizzy. "I can't. It's happening."

Veronica pushed a button beside the door, and curtains descended between the shelves and the windows. She pulled the one down over the door as well. With only the iridescent lights—she'd not used the ceiling fluorescents—the sense of twilight increased the urge. I fumbled for my shirt buttons, but my hands wouldn't—couldn't—obey. I dropped to all fours and crawled behind the counter.

"Veronica, undress me," I gasped.

"My arthritic fingers can't handle your little buttons. He'll have to do it."

Oh, gods, this isn't how I imagined this would happen.

"What?" Jared asked.

My skin tingled. "You need to help me out of my clothes. And hurry."

I didn't have time to think about the swiftness with which he undressed me—as if he got women out of their clothes all the time—but I did appreciate his gentleness in spite of his hands trembling. With desire or revulsion, I don't know, but I appreciated it. Then he stepped back, leaving me alone and naked, and I'm sure covered in a full-body blush of shame mixed with desire.

"Now what?" he asked. His voice sounded far away.

"We wait," Veronica said. "You can't watch the change—that's only reserved for those whom the lycanthrope trusts absolutely."

He moved from behind the counter. Then it happened, the pushing, pulling, prodding agony of transformation that the full moon gave force and swiftness. I panted on the floor of the counter and noticed his scent and mine mingling on my clothes. The sensation sparked my desire for him into a flame, and I decided that even if disappointment ensued, it was worth it to have him just once.

I trotted out from behind the counter. The stones on the shelves glowed, each with their own spirit and color, but none as brightly or as enticingly as Jared's eyes, which to my wolf vision sparked emerald green.

"Is that her?" he asked. To his credit, he'd stepped in front of Veronica as if to protect her from whatever I'd turned into. I appreciated his instinct even if his lack of trust in me hurt. But then, I was a wild animal.

"It is. She is." Veronica moved around him. "May I touch you?" she asked me.

I nodded and couldn't help but sniff her offered hand. I'd never smelled magic before. Hers had an earthy scent, like the ground after a good rain woke the roots and seeds.

As for Jared, he smelled like a gathering thunderstorm that needed release in a dramatic display of lightning and sheets of rain.

Speaking of sheets...

But I couldn't follow the thought because Veronica placed her hand on my head. I flinched away from it at first, but with a huff, allowed her. No one had touched me when I was a wolf, not even members of my pack, but I understood that she needed to in order to show Jared I was no threat.

Well, not in the biting sense, unless he was into that sort of thing.

"She's still Kyra even though she is a gorgeous wolf," Veronica said. "She has a different kind of magic almost as powerful as yours."

He moved around me, careful not to step on my tail, and looked behind the counter. Veronica moved her hand from my head, and I stifled a growl. Then he stood in front of me, and I looked up at him.

"Kyra, is that you?" he asked. There was a sense of wonder

to his voice, but he shifted his weight to his back leg as though preparing to jump back.

I nodded, then decided to try and see if I could telepathically speak to him like I had when he'd projected into Nona's house.

"It's me. I'm the same wolf you saw last night in your dream."

His quick intake of breath told me he'd heard me. "How is this possible?" he asked.

"Is she speaking to you? If so, let her." Veronica moved to sit behind the counter. She sounded weary.

"You can't hear her?" he asked.

"No, she is speaking only to you."

He knelt in front of me.

"You may touch me," I said.

He reached out a hand, then drew it back. "Are you sure?"

"Yes. Please touch me."

Even his dimples when he smiled seemed magical to me in my state. "I thought you'd never ask."

He ran his fingers lightly over my head and down my back. I wanted to lick him but thought that would be too dog-like, even if I wanted to taste him. Then he ran his hand over the soft fur of my throat and chest, and I did get a quick swipe of my tongue in. He tasted of the ocean salt with the sweetness of rainwater underneath.

"Kyra, we're about to have company," Veronica warned.

I pulled away from Jared's questing touch.

"We'll continue this later," I promised him.

"I'll hold you to that," he murmured.

"And you."

"I'm counting on it."

Veronica moved out of the way and allowed me to change back behind the counter. I had just re-dressed and was putting on my shoes when three knocks came at the door.

"Miss Chalice?" a voice called. I recognized the policeman from the day before.

"In a moment!" She turned to me. "Are you all right, dear?"

"I think so. Are you?" I asked Jared.

He grinned. "I definitely am. That was amazing. I had no idea you were a woman of such talent."

"Oh, you have no idea."

Veronica opened the door, and the young cop came in with two others. "We need to bring you down to the station for more questioning, ma'am. We've found evidence that your former employee, Miss Crystal LaForge, was poisoned."

10

UNDRESSING THE TRUTH

"Is this an arrest?" Jared asked.

The policeman turned to him, and his eyes widened. "Um, no sir, she's simply a person of interest."

"Regardless, I'm going to arrange for her to have legal counsel with her." He pulled his phone from his pocket.

Before he could call, Veronica said, "That will not be necessary, although I appreciate your offer of help."

"It's not just for you," he told her, but his gentle tone took the bite from his words. "Although I'm in no way involved, and neither is Kyra, it's best for everyone if we go ahead and have legal advice from the beginning."

At my name, the policemen whispered among themselves.

"What is it?" Jared asked.

"We got a tip that she might be involved as well."

"That's ridiculous. And she's not feeling well, so she can't go with you today." He called, and after a few short exchanges, hung up. "One of my attorneys will meet you at the station, Veronica."

The policemen's eyes had widened with each word, and I suspected they feared being turned into newts less than Jared's legal counsel. I couldn't do much, just sit on the stool and watch.

"I can take care of the store," I told her.

"Don't worry about it, you're too exhausted. Go on, and I'll close up and then accompany these gentlemen to the station."

I was too worn out from the change—my second in twenty-four hours—to argue. When we walked outside, I noticed clouds had gathered, and a cool breeze pricked my exposed skin. Jared walked beside me, his jawline tense.

"Is this you?" I asked as quietly as I could.

He looked up. "I have no idea." He rubbed his temples, and he looked as tired as I felt. We walked back to Nona's house slowly, and the fresh air cleared my head somewhat, but I was glad to reach the front door and take my shoes off.

"What now?" Jared asked.

I sighed. As much as I had enjoyed our day together, I knew it would have to end sometime. My mood had dropped with the temperature outside. Although Jared had an appreciation for novelty, now that he'd had the chance to think about my secret and ponder how it could interfere with a normal relationship, I couldn't imagine he would feel anything but revulsion for me. Or worse, a sick curiosity.

"I suppose you should return to Boston. Or didn't you say you had a business thing you needed to take care of up here?"

He didn't edge away, pull out his keys, or make any other motions like he wanted to leave. Instead, he took off his jacket, hung it on one of the hooks by the door, and bent to remove his shoes as well.

"What are you doing?" I asked.

"Getting ready to take care of a certain piece of business." He straightened, and his grin was so wide it showed both dimples. "My business was to come up here and find out what you know about the Fortunas."

"Not much," I said. And in truth, I didn't have much solid knowledge, just assumptions and hearsay.

"And now that's established, I can focus on other things."

He picked me up—literally swept me off my feet—and I had to hang on around his neck.

"First let's make sure the coast is clear," he said with a wink.

"From what?"

"Oh, intruders, ghosts…" He winked, but I glanced at Nona's pictures as we passed and tried not to feel that her dark eyes in each of them looked at me with judgment.

But if we kept things innocent, she wouldn't appear, right?

There was no crash from the kitchen, and we found it just as we left it. He placed me on the island and left me to look in the fridge.

"Hmmm, so you've been living on water and protein bars," he said. "That makes for a balanced diet."

"Totally." I ignored his facetiousness and admired his ass as he bent to look lower and open the empty vegetable crisper.

"And not a real vegetable in sight." He straightened and looked at me with a cocked eyebrow. Then he came to stand in front of me, trapping me between his hands, which he flattened on either side of me. I ran my fingers over his muscular arms.

"So what do you eat, wolf-girl?"

I stiffened. He was still there in spite of having seen what I would become every twenty-nine days, but I wasn't prepared for him to talk so casually about it.

"I haven't had time to go to the store," I said. "So I've had to make do with what I had on hand and what the kindness of strangers has brought me."

"You need some real food." He leaned closer.

"That's not really what I'm hungry for," I murmured.

"Oh, really?"

"Not vegetables." I grinned. "But I could totally do five a day."

He bent over with his laugh, and I missed the feel of his hands under my thighs. "That was horrible."

I widened my eyes innocently. "We were talking about vegetables."

The rolling pin, which had been secure in its cradle, rolled toward me and tapped my butt. I scooted off the island and glared at it.

"Right," I said. "No canoodling between unmarried couples."

His expression sobered, and he eyed the rolling pin like it was going to fly up and hit him. "So that part of my dream or whatever it was holds true—we're being watched."

"Always." I sighed. "As you can probably imagine, my brothers and I didn't have much in the way of summer romances up here."

"What, you didn't go to the Cape like normal people?"

The rolling pin turned a hundred and eighty degrees, and he pushed me behind him. "Is that thing dangerous?"

"No, but Nona is sensitive about that. She never liked Cape Cod in the summer. Too many city people, she said."

"Right. How about I order us some takeout, and then we can just watch television?"

The rolling pin rolled back to its cradle and bumped against it.

"I think that sounds good, and so does she." I walked around the island and put the wandering kitchen implement back in its little stand. "I'll be good, I promise," I said once Jared had left the kitchen to get a better cell signal with which to look up restaurants that would deliver. "But he is the world's most eligible bachelor, so if you could give me a little room to maneuver, that would be great."

One of the cabinets opened, and a box of powdered milk dropped to the counter.

"Message received," I said and put it back.

Jared ordered a vegetarian pizza—our compromise for how to get some vegetables into me—and he said at least I would have leftovers. I promised him I'd go to the store after work the next day.

After we ate, we'd watched a couple of on-demand episodes of *Charmed*. We both appreciated the irony, but I hoped I wouldn't have to deal with any of the weird nastiness the sisters did. I stopped him before he could move on to another episode.

"I should go to bed," I said with a sigh. "I'll be opening, I'm exhausted from changing today, and I'll need any extra energy I can muster for the full moon change tomorrow night."

I'd tossed out verbal tidbits about my problem all evening to see if he would balk, and he never had. It seemed kind of unfair that he got to do cool things with water, air, and energy, and I was stuck turning into an extra hairy bitchy mess every twenty-nine days.

"Are you sure you'll have work tomorrow?" he asked.

"Why wouldn't I?" I leaned back and looked at him with a frown. "I had planned to open, and I can be there all day and close if I need to."

He rubbed the back of my neck, and I returned to my former position with my back against the couch cushions and his arm behind me, but kept the regulation Catholic school two inches between my breasts and his chest. I wasn't sure if that was the right distance, but no crash ensued from the kitchen, so I figured it was close enough. Or far enough for the Holy Spirit to get in there. Like it didn't have anything better to do.

He glanced at his phone, which was on the couch on the other side of him. I'd ignored the texts he'd received and sent during the evening. There hadn't been that many, but enough to make me wonder if there was a jealous woman on the other end of them.

"The attorney I sent, Bill, says it doesn't look good for your friend even though they don't have any solid evidence against her. There wasn't any sign of forced entry, so they think the perpetrator was someone the girl knew."

"What about suicide?" I asked.

"Bill said they weren't saying why, but they've seemed to rule it out. Even if Veronica is innocent, all this could be enough to get her work visa pulled and her sent back to Scotland."

"Which would mean her sister could lose the store if she's not there to manage it."

"And you couldn't do it?"

"I can fill in, but I don't know enough of the nuances of the business to step in and manage it. Besides, this is just a temporary thing while—" I almost said While I get back on my feet, but I hadn't trusted him with that secret yet.

"While what?" He kneaded the tense spot on the top of my left shoulder.

I sighed and tried to relax under his touch, but I couldn't. I wanted the conversation to be over, but I didn't want him to stop touching me. I couldn't remember the last time a man had been so concerned for my comfort or well-being.

"It's okay," he said. "I get it—you're down on your luck because of your illness. I figured as much. Crystal shop girl isn't what I'd had in mind when you said you were here for a business opportunity."

"I'm sorry I lied," I told him. "I was embarrassed, and we'd only just reconnected." I couldn't believe it had been the day before. So much had passed since I'd fallen at his feet at the airport it felt like the incident had happened several weeks prior.

"It's fine, as long as you don't do it again. I can't help but think that if you had still been in your former life, you wouldn't have given me the time of day. You'd've just told me to fuck off, and I wouldn't have seen you again."

I drew back in surprise but put a hand on his arm. "I wouldn't have!" But he had a point. If I'd had more resources, I might have let my temper get the better of me. I certainly wouldn't have gone back to his condo with him.

Crap, I don't know whether to be more embarrassed by how I was or my circumstances now.

He drew a thumb along my cheek. "Don't be upset. It's all right. I'm glad I found you again."

"Me, too." I kissed his palm. He moved his hand to cup my head and drew me to him. We both hesitated, but nothing odd happened, so I closed the distance.

I had the sensation of cresting a wave with a heart-stopping drop followed by the exhilaration of the rush to shore, like flying but cradled by warmth. I parted my lips, wanting more, and he moved his other hand to rest on my hip. Another wave brought me to straddle him and fist my hands in his shirt.

The volume of the television increased, and we drew apart.

He turned it off and held up both hands as I scrambled off his lap.

"I think that's my signal," he said.

"Sadly, yes. Your place next time?" I whispered.

"I'm counting on it. Tomorrow night?"

"I can't. I have a date with my furry side," I said with a pout.

"We'll figure something out." He pecked me on the cheek, and I followed him into the foyer and watched him put on his shoes and jacket. He gave me a kiss on the lips that was over too soon, and I leaned against the door jamb and watched him drive away.

"I hope you will this time," I said after his tail lights had disappeared.

He'd seemed fine, but there was no telling what he'd decide after he thought about my situation for a while. Would he think

I was a gold-digger? Or would he be repulsed once the full implication of my illness's manifestation hit him?

Yes, there was chemistry between us, but he was a savvy businessman, and I suspected he could easily allow his head to overrule his heart.

As for me, I didn't know what to think or hope for. I cleaned up the kitchen and straightened the living room, but I was restless. There had to be something I could do for Veronica and her sister. I hadn't been modest when I told Jared I didn't think I could manage the store. If Veronica's sister was so ill she needed Veronica there, it meant she couldn't be in the shape needed to train and supervise a new manager. I'd never done retail, and the thought of ordering inventory I knew nothing about made me cringe.

My phone rang, and I answered without looking, thinking that maybe Jared was coming back and would invite me to hang out with him in some cute little bed and breakfast, where we could—

"Hey, Kyra, it's Cindy."

"Oh, hey." I tried to sound happy to hear from her. "Jared's on his way back to Boston."

"Oh, no. Did things not go well with you two?"

I almost held the phone out and looked at it disbelievingly. "Things are fine. I just thought you might be worried about him."

She laughed, and I imagined her dismissive hand wave. "No, not at all. He can take care of himself. I wanted to talk to you."

"What about?"

"It's too complicated to go into now. Can you meet for lunch tomorrow?"

"I'm not sure."

"Okay, just let me know. I'll be up there, anyway, so it'll be easy for me to pop by for a quick lunch and chat whenever you're available. Jared wants me to help him scout out potential commercial space."

We said our goodbyes and hung up. I couldn't figure out why she was so interested in me or what she wanted to talk to me about. But then, Jared seemed to be attracted to me, so maybe it was a sibling thing, and she wanted to check me out. I'd never done that for my brothers, but they and I weren't that close.

Meanwhile, too much energy coursed through my nerves for me to sleep.

Maybe the police missed something at Crystal's place that a wolf could smell. It seemed a long shot, but the moon already sang in my blood, and despite my efforts to the contrary, a strange giddiness kept making me smile when I thought about Jared's kisses. The two combined would mean a sleepless night unless I truly wore myself out.

A quick internet search showed me the address and directions for where I needed to go. Now all I had to do was figure out how to get out of the house.

A memory tickled my brain, that Nona had once had a dog. If I closed my eyes, I could picture where the dog went in and out, and it wasn't the kitchen. There was a door off the laundry room that had stuff piled around it, but I found what I thought I remembered—a doggy door. Not ideal, but necessary.

I made sure the rest of the house was locked up, took off my clothes, folded them on top of the dryer, and changed.

11

NOCTURNAL WANDERINGS

Crystal had lived in a duplex close to the main Salem State University campus. I wasn't sure what I thought I would find, but I did feel better after loping through the shadows and chasing a few nocturnal critters. I didn't stop to catch and eat any, but my wolf senses were satisfied by the chase.

Different scents assailed me on my trip—the brine of the air, the bitter scent of fallen leaves, and the plastic of the Halloween and festival decorations. But when I arrived at my target address, I found a smell both new and familiar—the same green, floral scent that had been in my kitchen. It was most concentrated around the back door of the duplex, and I wished I could get in and sniff around. Not that I would be able to find anything, and I knew better than to disturb a crime scene, but still, I wanted to do something.

Then it occurred to me—as a wolf, I could follow the more recent scent trail from my own kitchen door to see where it led.

First I trotted back and forth across the yard to see if anything of the trail from two days before lingered. There were areas here and there, but one spot in particular intrigued me.

Apparently whoever it was had stood there for a while, and when I walked over it, the ground felt different, barely softer. A human in shoes wouldn't have noticed it, but I did with my bare paws.

A noise made me look up, and I saw the same teenager from the store that afternoon. No, not her, but one who looked very like her, except she was dressed in seventeenth-century costume like one of the witch girls in the museum dioramas. She disappeared, and I shook my head to clear the ringing echo in my ears. The encounter had been brief enough to make me question my perception but strong enough that my fur stood on end. I made a quick note of the spot in the yard and returned to the street, where I felt I could breathe again.

I backtracked to my grandmother's house and found what I was looking—er, smelling—for. The trail led to the north, opposite the direction of Crystal's duplex and straight to the commons and the galleria where Veronica's shop was.

This perplexed me. I knew Veronica wasn't the perpetrator —presumably she'd been working when whoever it was had broken into my grandmother's house—and she didn't have the right scent, anyway.

Voices alerted me to someone coming, and I ducked between a garbage can and a wall, hoping I'd blend in. The smells of melted cotton candy and rancid-turning festival food made me want to hold my breath.

"I know you're jet-lagged, but this can't wait," Veronica was saying to a man and a woman following her. The woman wore a hat and a coat with a turned-up collar that kept me from seeing her face clearly.

The man, who had reddish-blond hair, yawned. "I slept on the plane, but Lonna didn't."

"Couldn't," the woman said, and my ears flattened at the sound of her name and her voice. I remembered standing on the front porch of a grand old manor house and arguing with her and then Matt telling me I needed to get out because I'd been accused of impersonating her to get her fired.

Veronica held a hand up, and the three stopped. I silenced the low growl that had emerged and tried not to do anything that would further draw attention to me.

"*Who's there?*" Lonna's mental voice came to me, and I tried to think of darkness and nothing else, but the image of the disdainful look she'd given me flashed through my brain.

"Kyra?" she asked out loud.

"Ah." Veronica looked straight at me. "Come on out, you're caught."

The man, who I'd figured out was Max Fortuna, looked amused. "So this is the infamous Kyra Ellison."

I came out from behind the trash can with my tail between my legs. If I'd been in human form, I would have been afire with a blush.

"You might as well come in, too," Veronica said. "I have a robe you can borrow, and then we'll all talk."

After changing in the store behind the desk again, I put on Veronica's robe and called out, "Okay, I'm decent."

The robe smelled of Veronica—damp earth, fresh night air, and the sharpness of flint. It was too bad I couldn't tell the police she had the wrong layers of scent to be the perpetrator. Then I'd probably be locked up for a different reason.

They came in, and we sat in a circle. Veronica closed the door and murmured something, and the sound of something snapping into place made me jump.

"Good concealment spell," Max said with an approving nod.

"Thank you. I can only do it with the aid of the crystals. I promise this won't take long," she said.

"What about her?" Lonna asked and inclined her head to me. She was still lovely, if tired-looking. I remembered that feeling, of being off an international flight and wanting nothing more than a shower and a bed but having to go to one more meeting, and I almost felt sorry for her.

"I suspect she is here because she has information that's relevant to what I called you about," Veronica said.

"The murder or the weather wizard?" Max pulled out his phone. "Kurt and Merlin will be here in the morning to take him into custody."

I stood. "No!"

All eyes turned toward me.

"You can't do anything to him," I said. "He's a free citizen of the United States of America. You can't just arrest him."

"He's potentially dangerous." Lonna cocked her head and fixed me with a measuring look. "Do you have some sort of relationship with him?"

I only glared at her. She'd falsely accused me of something in the past, so I wasn't going to give her the satisfaction of something else she could use against me.

"There is some mutual interest, but also a lot of fear," Veronica said. "But that is not important at the moment." She looked at Max and Lonna. "Neither is the weather wizard himself. He is untrained, only coming into what he can do, but there is a greater danger."

"What?" Lonna cut her eyes to me.

I returned my gaze to her, and we sat in challenge until Max said, "Enough."

My tip twitched, and I caught myself before I bared my teeth. "What is your problem with me?" I asked Lonna. "I haven't done anything to you, yet the pack thinks I did."

"What do you mean?" She looked genuinely confused.

"They think I impersonated you to try to get you fired from your job. Former job. As a social worker."

"Oh." She shook her head, and her cheeks turned pink. "I did ask about you, but that ended up being something completely different. I ended up leaving the country before I could go back and explain."

I crossed my arms and sat. "Leaving them thinking I was trying to hurt you. I got kicked out of our pack."

"I am truly sorry," she said. "There was some strange metaphysical stuff going on. I never actually accused you of anything, just asked where you were because something odd had happened to me, and we somewhat resemble each other."

I wanted to be angry, but I was too tired. "Whatever you say. You're here now, so you need to help me with the current situation. Someone's after Veronica. And me."

She nodded and at least had the sense to look abashed. "I agree, and I'll call Matt in the morning and straighten things out."

"Thank you."

Max cleared his throat. "Veronica, is that what you meant by something more urgent—that you're in danger?"

The panicked look he gave her made me wonder why he should be so concerned about one frumpy, albeit talented witch. It only confirmed what I suspected—that she was here for more reason than to help her ill sister with the shop.

"Yes. Someone is trying to interfere with my mission. That one—" she pointed to me "—has sniffed it out, so to speak. That's another reason I wanted you to come." Now she took on a frightening aspect, her eyes dark. "So you could interrogate her and wipe her memory if she's not trustworthy."

"Uh." I stood again. "Well, this has been fun, but I should be going."

"Sit," Veronica said, and my knees buckled, bringing my ass down hard on the chair. "Maximilian, go ahead and test her."

12

REVELATIONS II

I tried to move, but my limbs hung leaden in the chair. I recalled that Crystal had been poisoned. Had someone slipped something to me? The only person who could have was Jared, and I didn't think it was him. Or I hoped not.

"Don't fight it," Lonna said. "You have a witch, a wizard, and a wizard-werewolf hybrid magically holding you in place."

"Who's the freak?" I asked through clenched teeth.

"I prefer the term truly unique individual," she said with a small smile. "Although there are more of us than you'd suspect. Max?"

"Right." He stood and put a hand on my head. "One has already died, and others—likely including yourself—are in danger. Consequently, the information you hold could save your life as well as those of others. Do you consent to this interrogation?"

"Well, when you put it like that..." Nope, still couldn't move. "Do I have a choice?"

"Always." The shadows under his eyes had deepened, and it seemed to pain him to have to do whatever he was doing to me.

I didn't have anything to hide, but I hated what this had

come to. But Jared was also in danger. If I could do something to get in their good graces and then leverage that to help him, I'd cooperate.

"I consent, but only on one condition."

Max raised his eyebrows. "What?"

"That you will cure me if you have, indeed, found the remedy for CLS."

He sighed. "I can't promise you that because while we're close, we're not quite there. We're still testing what we have and working out the kinks."

"So the leak wasn't accurate." The little part of me that had expected to be disappointed sent a jolt of *I told you so* bitterness through my gut.

"No, but I promise to keep you apprised of our progress. Will that work?"

"Sure."

"Good. First, what do you know of the Lycanthrope Council?"

"Not a whole lot, only that they're in Scotland."

He nodded. "Good. And what about the Institute for Lycanthropic Reversal?"

"Only that you've managed to come up with a cure for lycanthropy, or that you're close." My tongue tripped along. "But there are those who don't think it should be cured and those who feel the remedy should be available to everyone, even those born with CLS."

He continued to ask me questions, and my mouth moved of its own accord, sometimes saying things that had been outside my awareness until he asked about them. Then we got to the strange spot I'd discovered outside of Crystal's apartment.

Lonna leaned forward. "The ground was different? Like how? Like someone buried something?"

Max removed his hand from my head and shook it.

"That's all I can do," he said.

I glanced up, then away. He hadn't asked me about Jared, for which I was thankful. At least he had kept his questions limited to the murder and respected my personal privacy.

Or maybe my relationship with Jared—if it could even be called a relationship—didn't matter in the grand scheme of things.

I chose to answer Lonna's question even though I was no longer compelled. "It's hard to explain. It's more like the dirt was a different type."

"Protected, perhaps." Veronica drummed her fingers on her thigh. "We should take a look at it."

"You shouldn't." Lonna stood and stretched. "You're a person of interest in a murder, remember? If you're found there, it will only hurt your case. Kyra, I know you're exhausted from your changing, but can you lead us there?"

"She needs to be careful, too," Veronica said with a sigh. "A tip has associated her with the murder."

The thought made my bones ache preemptively, but I knew what needed to be done. "I can take you and show you the spot on one condition."

"What?" Max asked.

"You have your people leave Jared alone."

Max rubbed his eyes. "All right, but I at least need to talk to him."

I tried not to grin too widely, but the pieces to solve my own puzzles were falling into place nicely. If I could arrange for Jared to talk to Max and Lonna without being in danger from the wizards, he could get the cure for CLS. Then I'd have an excuse to spend more time with him and be a test subject, too. Perhaps then I'd have the chance at a normal professional and personal life.

I walked behind the counter. "Just give me a moment to change."

THE CHANGE so exhausted me that Max and Lonna allowed me to crash out in the backseat of their rental car. It felt like I had just drifted off to sleep when we arrived at the crime scene tape-surrounded duplex, and I shook myself awake.

Veronica had loaned them some shovels from the fool's gold display in her store, for which I was glad. I didn't think I had the strength to dig. I showed them the spot, and Max held up a hand before Lonna could lower her shovel. I looked around, and my fur stood on end. It felt like something watched us.

"There's something strange here, a spell or something that makes this the most uninteresting spot in the yard to a wizard." He cleared the fallen leaves, and I sniffed, but all I could smell was the mixture of sharp autumn decay and dampness characteristic of leaves that had been on the ground for a while.

"Can you detect anything?" he asked me and Lonna.

"No," Lonna said and knelt. Her nostrils flared, and I guessed she was trying to get her inner wolf to come out.

Something brushed past me, and I jumped back at the sight of another black wolf that didn't have a scent. My lips curled in a snarl.

"It's okay," Max said. "Lonna's inner wolf is sometimes an outer wolf, sort of a guardian spirit."

"Can she change, too?" I asked, fascinated.

"Yes," Lonna said, and her voice echoed through the other wolf, which sniffed at the spot.

"There is something dangerous to lycanthropes, but it is buried. The wolves should stand back," it said and then vanished.

"She's useful like that," Lonna told me. "Let's stand over there."

I didn't want to stand near the woods, where the shadows gathered, and I glanced around while Max dug.

Finally he unearthed a metal box. He opened it and pulled

out a sheaf of papers and an envelope. He rubbed his fingers together.

"It's bank statements and some sort of powder. Veronica said Crystal was poisoned, right?"

"Yes."

He stood. "I'm going to call my contacts here and get them to rush the autopsy. Lonna, take Kyra back to her place. I'll walk back to town with this stuff. I don't want you anywhere near it."

"Will you be all right?" she asked.

"Your wolf said it was dangerous to you, not to me. I'll take it to Veronica's place. Meet me there."

He replaced the dirt in the hole and covered it with leaves.

Lonna took me back to my place without saying much. She didn't have to—she emanated worry.

"He's a powerful wizard and can take care of himself," she said as she pulled up to my place. "But there are others." She turned to look at me where I lay in the backseat. "You did well with the interrogation, and again, I'm sorry for whatever I said to make the others kick you out. This is a strange time for all of us, and a lot of wizards and lycanthropes oppose what we're doing at the ILR. Be very careful about who you trust."

With that, she let me out of the car. I went back in through the laundry room doggie door, and, still in wolf form, crawled up the stairs and into bed. My change back into human felt like a bad dream.

~

I woke around midday with my hand on my phone, having apparently shut off my primary, secondary, and final backup alarms.

I'm late for work! But when I sat, the room tilted, and I fell back. At some point during the night, I'd pulled the covers over me, so the bed was a muddy, gritty mess. Everything that was human about me wanted a shower and clean sheets, but my leaden limbs barely permitted me to move.

I pushed myself up and swung my feet toward the floor. That effort made my heart race, and I took a couple of deep breaths to slow it and the room's seasickness-inducing motion. I wondered if I could make it to the bathroom should the nausea worsen.

The phone beeped with an incoming text, and the jolt of panic nearly cleared the lethargic sensation—*Jared! The wizards are coming for him. But didn't I buy him more time?*

Even so, I needed to warn him.

The text was from him, and some of the tension in my chest released.

Need to see you, he said. Fortuna in States. Expedited autopsy. (!)

Can't—have flu, I texted back. *Don't want you to get sick. Watch out for wizards.*

OMW. Not flu. Danger. Call Veronica.

I blinked, and it felt like I burned at least a hundred calories with the effort.

What do u mean? But he didn't answer, so I suspected he was already in his car.

Making a phone call seemed beyond my capabilities. I prioritized and decided a quick shower would have to come first with the hope it would help me feel better and the steam would make my head stop pounding.

I managed to clean myself up and stagger downstairs for some water. Part of my brain knew that fluids were good, but I didn't want to deal with whatever grittiness was in the water pitcher, so I grabbed a bottle of water from the pantry. The only food was leftover pizza, of course, and the thought of cold cheese and vegetables made me feel more ill.

I went into the living room and curled up under the afghan my grandmother had crocheted for the couch a decade before. I couldn't get a hug from her, so it would have to do.

"Nona, if you're here, help me," I whispered.

No reply came.

The chills from the illness raced through my body along with the electric echoes of the full moon. This one, being soon before Halloween, would be powerful. I'd never been sick during a mandatory change time before. In fact, I'd been oddly healthy with not even a cold since developing CLS.

A knock on the front door roused me from the half-dream state I'd been in. The disturbing images of something after me but being unable to run faded, but the feeling of something being horribly wrong didn't. I shambled to the front door—seriously, I could've been a zombie movie extra without any makeup—and opened it to see not Jared, but Cindy.

"Kyra, what's wrong?"

She moved to come in, but I held up a hand.

"I'm really sick. I'm sorry, I can't do lunch today."

She put a hand over her mouth and nodded. Her eyes flicked to something over my shoulder, and she paled. I turned to look behind me but didn't see anything.

With a, "Don't worry, we'll reschedule. Feel better!" she rushed away and got in her car, which she'd backed into the driveway. I thought I saw someone sitting in the passenger seat, but the angle of the sun made it hard to make out details, and I dismissed the impression to my brain being foggy.

I stood there for a while like an idiot because the thought of going back, lying down, and then having to get up to answer the door again exhausted me. Finally I closed the door and lay in the front hallway, still wrapped in the afghan, which now felt like a robe of protection, although I couldn't say why.

It was a good thing, considering I hadn't locked the door, although I thought I remembered that I had, and I woke to the concerned face of Max Fortuna looming over me.

"Go away, you'll get sick," I said.

"Doubtful," Max told me. "And I'm here to help. I can't remember if I mentioned I'm a doctor."

He helped me to sit and then walk into the living room. I noticed an old-fashioned doctor's bag by the front door. I appreciated the old-school touch, although I wanted him to go away so Jared could come and safely take care of me without being detained.

"What's going on?" I asked.

"The powder in the box last night wasn't a poison. It was an attempt at a cure for Chronic Lycanthropy Syndrome. That's what the young lady died from—she was a lycanthrope like you."

"And I'm sick from being exposed to it? Is Lonna okay?"

"Yes," Max said. "The powder has to be ingested." He ran a hand through his hair. "Can you think of any way it could have gotten into your system?"

"No."

"By the way, do you have any water? I've been weakened by the travel, interrogation, and the magic I had to work this morning and need to rehydrate."

"I have bottles, and there's a pitcher in the fridge." I grimaced remembering the sand in the pitcher.

Or maybe it hadn't been sand.

"Wait!" I called after him, but he didn't seem to hear me. I staggered after him and found him pouring a glass of water from the pitcher.

I knocked the glass out of Max's hand, and it shattered on the floor. "Don't drink that! I think someone put the powder in the water pitcher."

13

THE GAME IS ON

I went back to the couch as Max cleaned the mess on the kitchen floor.

Don't come, I texted Jared. *Trap.*

Are you all right?

I didn't want to lie, but I suspected that if I were to tell him the truth, he'd end up captured or worse.

Fine for now. I curled up again and wished I could stop shivering in spite of being wrapped in the blanket.

"Can you help me?" I asked when Max returned. He had the doctor's bag with him.

"Let me get some vitals. I don't know exactly what's going on with you, only that systemic changes are trying to happen." He took my blood pressure and temperature, and he listened to my heart and lungs.

"Tachycardia," he murmured. "Fever. Diaphoresis."

"Listen to you with your fancy big words," I said so I wouldn't blurt out what I really thought—*Either help me or go away.*

"Listen to you with your sarcasm." He smiled. "You don't have to worry about Jared, by the way."

"You're going to leave him alone?"

"No, but it will be better for him if he comes to get trained. And the rest of the world. Power that's not used properly can be harmful to the bearer and recipients." He looked at me with an expression I could only describe as deadly serious. "Trust me, I know."

I didn't take the bait to ask him what he meant. I was sick, not stupid, and I wouldn't be diverted. "That needs to be his choice. It's unfair enough that he's been saddled with this. He can't be expected to just give up everything and embrace a strange new life he knows nothing about."

"And you would know what that's like."

"Yes, I would." I would have given him my haughtiest look if I'd had the energy. "Now are you going to help me or not?"

"Give me your phone."

"What?" I cradled it against me.

"Just give it to me." He held his hand out.

"Fine." It was locked, so he shouldn't be able to—

He waved a hand over it, and it unlocked. The air around it shimmered like the kitchen had the previous day when someone had magically locked the door behind them.

"Give that back!" I lunged for it, but he was able to push me away with a gentle hand on my chest. He made a call.

"Jared Steel?"

I glared at him.

"Yes, this is Max Fortuna. Kyra is very ill. She's been exposed to the same thing that killed the girl from the shop." He paused. "No, a hospital won't do any good. She needs a powerful wizard to work a certain kind of magic, and I'm too depleted from the energy I had to expend on analyzing the powder to do it."

"Don't listen to him," I said, hoping he'd hear me. "Don't come. Don't lose your life and your freedom and..." I stifled a sob in the afghan.

"He's almost here," Max said. He handed the phone back to me. "I'm sorry, but you're being stubborn, and sacrificing yourself won't save him from what will happen eventually."

I tried to unlock my phone, but the battery was dead.

"Again, sorry." He shrugged. "I needed the extra energy to unlock it without the code."

I wanted to glare at him, but the room turned gray, and my eyelids descended like leaden curtains.

A knock on the door startled me, but I couldn't open my eyes. It was like a horrible nightmare where I was paralyzed, and all I could do was listen to the sound of Max going to answer the door and then voices in the hall.

"Kyra!" Jared took my hand. "Please say something."

"The substance is doing its work quickly," Max told him. "You need to clear it from her."

"But how?"

"I'm going to give you a trade secret you mustn't tell anyone. Part of the cure for Chronic Lycanthropy Syndrome is a bit of blood magic to give it a push. I suspect that something similar will help to pull this false cure back."

"So you'll do it?" Jared asked.

"I can't. Or I could, but I'm already drained from the day's exertions. I can instruct you, and you being close to her will help it work better. But I warn you, once you take this important step on the path toward becoming a wizard, you cannot turn back."

"Don't do it!" I yelled mentally. Physically I could only manage a whimper.

"I'll do whatever it takes to save her."

I felt something being stuck in my arm, and the darkness spread and took me under into a dreamless, formless sleep. Or maybe my body felt formless, as it did at that instant when I'm neither wolf nor human during my changes, but something in between that doesn't—shouldn't—exist.

I SLIPPED through the darkness into a state somewhere between lucid dreaming and vivid remembering.

The grand chandelier of a ballroom came into focus overhead, and when I dropped my gaze, I found I was at the Steel Pharmaceuticals holiday party of a few years previously. Jared had invited me as a fellow business owner in the Little Rock area and asked if I would bring some of my more outgoing girls to "talk to other party guests," which I knew was code for, "save me some potential drama and give the old men something to leer at besides each other's trophy wives," but I felt it was good for the girls to be seen in case someone wanted to hire one of them for a commercial or some other small job to build her portfolio.

The crystal glass of water sweated through the black napkin I had wrapped around it, telling me my temperature was rising again. I had just started showing what I thought was the flu but ended up being CLS transition symptoms, and I had promised myself I would only stay an hour. My time was up, and I looked for the party host so I could excuse myself.

I found Jared standing by a large chafing dish full of bacon-wrapped scallops, and he shook hands with the old gentleman he'd been talking to and turned to me.

"I just told Henry that you and I had urgent business to discuss," he said, speaking close to my ear as he took my elbow and steered me to a quiet corner. "Thank you for saving me. The man doesn't know when to talk business and when to enjoy himself."

"My pleasure," I said. Soothing calm radiated from his cool fingertips on my elbow. "But aren't you supposed to make major deals in smoky back rooms after parties like this once you dismiss the womenfolk?"

He grinned, and I had to smile back even though I felt like I had a heavy chafing dish on my chest. Now the cool of his hand moved up my arm to my shoulder, which was exposed in the sleeveless red floor-length sheath I'd worn.

"I suspect that a man would dismiss you at his peril," he told me and caressed my shoulder. "But enough flirting, although I could do that with you all night."

I could think of a few things I'd like to do all night with him, and I captured the tip of my tongue between my teeth so I wouldn't blurt that out.

"I'm concerned about you," he continued. "You haven't been your usual outgoing self, and you're very warm. Should I have the hotel staff lower the temperature in the room?"

He'd noticed me? We'd barely exchanged more than "Hello, nice to see you, thank you for inviting me," at previous parties.

"I'm afraid I'm not feeling well, and you're kind for noticing. I should collect the girls and go soon. I'm very sorry to take them away. Your friend Henry seems to have taken a liking to Brittany."

He glanced in the direction I indicated. "Oh, lord. Yes, you should probably rescue her, but I do have one question for you before you go. And please let me call a limo for you. You shouldn't be driving if you feel horrible."

"What's the question?" I gave him a classic female, "Are you interested in me?" look and thought I saw an answering smolder in his gaze.

But before he said anything, Cindy appeared at his elbow and touched his arm. He dropped his hand from my shoulder. No, it fell away as though struck senseless, and he blinked with a confused furrow between his eyebrows.

"It's time to start pouring for the toast," Cindy said. "Do you have your speech ready? Oh, hello, Miss Ellison, I'm glad you could join us."

I wanted to tell her she'd interrupted us, but I was too polite, and Jared seemed dazed.

"It was lovely to see you," he told me and followed his sister away.

A full-body chill overtook me, and somehow I got home. I think one of my girls brought me. I'd gone into a full change the next night, and I'd forgotten everything about the incident at the party except that we'd had a nice conversation, and I'd thought he would call to ask me out later. My breakdown kept us from any further social encounters.

So had Cindy had anything to do with it? She'd seemed so friendly recently. Maybe she wanted to make up for it and put me and Jared back together?

My questions floated to the surface of consciousness with me, but they popped like bubbles when I opened my eyes.

JARED SAT ON THE FLOOR, still holding my hand. When he saw me looking at him, he smiled.

"How are you feeling?"

I stretched, and the heaviness was gone. My head felt clearer than it had in weeks, and my stomach growled.

"Hungry. How are you?"

"Exhausted. We have one night together before I have to report to the wizards for training. But the good news is that once I'm done, I can partner with the Fortunas and make the CLS cure here."

"With magic," I said, and I couldn't keep the distaste from my voice.

"With magic," he agreed. "Hey," he said and put a finger under my chin. "It saved your life."

"You saved my life," I told him. He leaned in to kiss me, and my stomach growled again.

"Let me guess, you haven't eaten today, have you?"

"Nope."

He stood and let go of my hand. "No canoodling until you get something in your stomach."

"It's not necessary." The words came out of my mouth before I could stop them. "I can hunt."

"Oh, right, tonight is your change."

"Don't worry," I said and stood. "You can cure me of that once you get trained. Then we can pick up again." I tried to sound supportive.

"I…" He shook his head. "I can't. Or I could, but we can't. Max told me that he and Lonna have a special dispensation from the Wizard Tribunal and Lycanthrope Council to be together. Wizards and lycanthropes aren't supposed to mix."

"What?" I crossed my arms against the chill that had come into the room. "That's ridiculous."

A tap on my shoulder made me turn, and I jumped when I saw Nona's ghost.

"There you are," I said. "Where were you earlier?"

"Protecting you."

"From what?"

"From those who would take you."

"Who?" But then I remembered. "Cindy?"

"My sister?" Jared asked.

Nona nodded. "Sometimes families harbor the worst betrayals. And there is more to your blood than you think, dear granddaughter. The Benandanti were both wizard and wolf before the laws of separation." She disappeared.

Before I could ponder what her words meant, Jared's phone rang. "It's Cindy," he said and answered it. "Heya, Cin. You're on speaker. I'm here with Kyra."

"Oh!" I could tell how surprised she was from that one syllable. "How are you feeling?"

"Much better."

"That's great. Hey, I'm still in Salem if you want to grab a late bite to eat."

"Thanks, but I've got plans."

Jared motioned for me to keep her talking.

"But if we're free later, would you like to meet up for a drink?"

"Oh, sure. There's a bar a little off the beaten path that's got a good cocktail list." She rattled off a name—The Purple Toenail—and an address. "Just text me and let me know when you're coming."

She hung up.

"That didn't sound suspicious at all," I said and plugged my phone into the charger I'd brought with me and set up in the living room. I had to keep moving because if I stilled, I would start to change, and I couldn't let him see me during my grotesque transformation.

"No." He frowned. "Did I tell you Cindy was the one who wanted me to come to Salem to meet you? She encouraged me after you ended up at my condo, said she could tell I was interested in you."

"No, you didn't mention that." I folded the afghan. The moonlight buzzed in my blood.

"And she had also bought a strange present for me, an antique book, but I only flipped through it."

"Wait, what?" I turned from the couch. "That's why you looked so odd when Veronica asked."

He nodded. "I didn't think anything of it, but things kept dragging me here to Salem, like the call about the murder." He rubbed his temples. "And we went to lunch, and we surprised whoever was putting the poison in your water pitcher. This is all too connected to be a coincidence, but I can't see it clearly."

"I'm sorry," I told him. "But I've really got to indulge my wolf side. Would you mind giving me a lift somewhere I can roam for an hour? That should do it for me."

It would be like an appetizer when I wanted a full meal, but it would have to do. I wanted to spend as much of our last allowed night together engaged in other animal activities.

"Of course."

"Great, I'll be down in a moment."

I went up to my bedroom and wished I was changing into something more comfortable. As it was, I hoped my fur coat was at least glossy after my illness of the day.

The power of the moon helped me to change smoothly, and I trotted downstairs. Jared stood by the front door with it open, and the scent from the mat hit me. It was the same scent from the kitchen—the clean, floral smell of a woman with mischief on her mind.

But the only female person who had stood there was Cindy.

"Jared, does your sister have any special talents like yours?"

"Not that I know of, but we haven't spent a lot of time together aside from recently."

"Does she have any reason to want to hurt you or the business?"

"No. In fact, she is a partner in addition to having her own small firm, so if the business does well, so does she."

His phone rang, and the screen showed who it was—Max. Jared answered it.

"I'm sorry to interrupt you on your special night," he said, "but I was just looking at the bank statements we dug up from the dead woman's yard, and there's a suspicious large transfer into her account. It turned out to be an offshore account for a company called CS Holdings. Isn't that your sister's investment company?"

"Yes," Jared said. "And I'm not sure whether to be more disturbed that you're able to rush autopsies and get through layers of financial security or that my sister is involved in this, which I'd already suspected."

"Energy wizards are great hackers. Do you know where she is?"

"Yes, she called me about getting together with her this

evening." He pinched the bridge of his nose, and I wished I could hug him or otherwise physically support him. I'd been hurt enough by my siblings' rejection, but none of them had ever betrayed me.

"Then we should probably find her before she decides to disappear."

14

AND THE WITCHES WATCH

We met Max, Lonna, and Veronica at the store. Lonna was in wolf form, and Max had a couple of extra wizards with him. I wondered if they would be the ones to whisk Jared away at the end of what was supposed to be our night together. It took all my human willpower to keep from baring my teeth at them.

"What's the battle plan?" Jared asked.

I gave him a baleful look. *"You stay out of the way and let the trained wizards handle this. Plus, Cindy is your sister. Do you really think you could hurt her?"*

He glanced around, then down at me. "When you talk in my head like that, I forget you're a wolf."

"With big, pointy teeth." I yawned to allow him a glimpse of them.

"And you should stay out of the way since you're recovering from the false cure," he told me.

I wanted to argue, but Max held up a hand. "We will likely all be needed, although Jared, you should not demonstrate what you can do. I don't want an international magical incident on my hands. You'll go talk to her. Kyra and Lonna, you wait in the shadows. Kurt, Merlin, and I will stick with Jared and apprehend her when it's time."

"How will we know it's time?" Jared asked, and then with a child in a Disney World commercial-sized grin, "Merlin?"

The wizard in question, who looked like he was in his mid-thirties but who smelled older—not in an old man sort of way, but rather a sun-warmed marble statue way—shrugged. "No relation to the famous one, I'm afraid," he said with an English accent.

Lonna and I exchanged glances. I could tell she didn't buy it, either, but neither of us said anything. If he was *the* Merlin, I would feel much better about the upcoming encounter.

"Remember," Max said, "we're dealing with someone who's already killed one person and would likely not hesitate to do so again. Plus, if Jared's abilities are any indication, they have very strong magic in their family. Be ready for anything."

No one spoke as we walked to The Purple Toenail. As promised, it was out of the way enough and through a sketchy enough area that we managed to shed the tourist crowds, which grew thicker as we approached Halloween itself.

We found Cindy sitting with a guy by a firepit on the patio. Another couple sat with them, and the air shimmered around all of them more than one would expect from the firelight.

"All wizards working some sort of magic," Lonna said. *"Max, be careful."*

"We will," he said. "Merlin, hang back so you're not caught if it is a trap."

"Aye." He disappeared into the shadows as though he had been born to them. Lonna and I exchanged another glance.

Cindy glanced at her watch, then out into the dark. The humans stood behind a wall, but Lonna and I crouched in the dark and could see everything. During a full moon change, our human eyesight augmented our wolf sight so we had the best of both and then some.

The three wizards approached the group on the patio. When Cindy saw Jared, she stood, her expression stricken.

"Omigod, is Kyra okay? Why isn't she with you? Did she take a turn for the worse?"

The trio on the patio who had been sitting with Cindy exchanged sly smiles, and I wanted to bite all of them.

"She's resting," he said. "I'm going to check on her later."

"Oh, good." But she sounded disappointed. "Who's this?"

Jared introduced Max and Kurt, and they all sat.

"So you're Maximilian Fortuna," Cindy said and stirred her drink. "Y'all had some big news recently. Are you looking for an American partner?"

"Yes," Max said. "But I'd rather discuss that privately, as we're still working out the kinks in the process. I have a place where you, Jared, and I could meet."

"Now?" Cindy gestured to the people she sat with. "I'm afraid I'm not in the best frame of mind to talk business. My friends and I have been having a good time. Why don't you join us, and we can talk in the morning?"

Jared's fist clenched under the table, but his expression remained neutral. Make that tired. I wondered what he'd done to me that afternoon. It seemed to have drained him, and being in the presence of the wizards appeared to make him fade faster in spite of his being outside.

"I'm afraid time is of the essence," Max told her. "A competitor here is already working on their own attempt at a cure."

"Oh?" She looked at him coyly. "And how would you know this?"

"Corporate secret, ma'am," the taciturn wizard named Kurt said.

"I see. Jared, could you join me for a second?" She rose and left the table. Jared followed her to the edge of the patio near where Lonna and I crouched.

"What is this?" she asked without any pretense of niceness. She touched him on the arm, and he tried to jerk back, but she held on. "Tell me."

The two words echoed in the air between them. His face took on a sheen of sweat.

"Oh, crap, she's a lock wizard," Lonna whispered in her mental voice. I barely registered this due to the effort it was taking to stay silent so Jared could keep Cindy talking.

"Why don't you tell me?" he ground out from his clenched jaw. "You pushed me toward Kyra and then tried to poison her."

"You mean cure her. I was doing it for you, dear brother, and your business."

"I don't believe you."

A chill, damp gust of wind ruffled her short blonde hair. She smoothed it with her free hand but kept hold of him. I recalled her touching him at the party where he forgot about me, or seemed to.

"I need to stop her. She's going to make him forget me again."

"Wait," Lonna told me. *"She can't wipe his memories, only lock them."*

Suddenly the strange events in my grandmother's kitchen made sense. *"Can she get into and out of locked houses?"*

"Yes. Is that how she poisoned you?"

"I think so. She put the stuff in my water pitcher."

"Stop fighting me, Jared," Cindy said. "If Kyra is ill, then either she will be cured or dead, and we don't need the ILR if the former is true. And if she dies..." She shrugged. "This is huge, and you don't need the distraction of a relationship."

"I'm allowed to have a life," Jared told her and jerked away. He scrubbed his hand over his face. "You stopped me from following up with her before after that one holiday party."

"You and Ted wouldn't let me have a boyfriend. Why should I let you have that happiness?"

"Now you're not making sense."

"Have you forgotten so soon, big brother, how ignored I was as a child, the surprise after the infertility-breaking miracle babies came along? The only time our parents paid attention to me was when I tried to forge my own identity, especially when I started dating. Our strange family curse meant any time I got serious about someone, one of you would show up and ruin it."

"We only responded when we felt you were in danger."

"In danger of what?" She got louder with each question. "Growing up? Ending up with a broken heart? Being my own person?"

"She's not making any sense, is she?" I asked Lonna. Admittedly, my brothers hadn't cared who I dated, or hadn't seemed to.

Lonna nudged me so I turned to her. She held my gaze as she said, *"That's what happens when a wizard isn't trained. The magic warps their mind."*

Hint taken – don't insist that the wizards leave Jared alone. With a shiver, I returned my attention to the scene.

The young man Cindy had been sitting with came over. "Is everything all right?" he asked with a French accent.

"Yes, Thierry. I was just telling my brother how things are going to be. Now, let's catch us an energy wizard who can show Jared how to do blood magic so we can make our own CLS cure."

Lonna sprang from the shadows, and, finally able to give voice to my anger, I followed with a snarl. I went for Cindy and Lonna for Thierry, but a gust of wind knocked me backwards, and Lonna and I tumbled into a furry heap. I looked up with surprise at Jared, but he frowned at the couple Cindy had been sitting with. Now they stood side-by-side with hands clasped and their free hands aimed at us.

"Air elementals," Max warned us, but it was too late—we were trapped by a swirling cage of wind.

"Ah, so there she is." Cindy picked herself up and peered

through the invisible wall that held me and Lonna. "She looks fine. What did you do to her, dear brother?" She stood and clapped her hands. "Did you manage to perform the magical step? No, because then she would be cured. But you did something. And the other wolf must be Lonna Marconi-Fortuna."

"Leave her alone," Max said. He tried to approach, but Thierry put up a hand, and Max stopped.

"You are not the only energy wizard here," Thierry said. "If you come closer, I will add lightning to their wind storm, and they will both perish."

"Um, can he do that?" I asked.

"'Fraid so."

Lonna and I huddled together inside our little whirlwind. The swirling air confused my nose with a myriad of scents under the overpowering ozone smell. A fog crept up and surrounded the porch.

"Is that you?" I asked Jared. He stood with arms crossed and eyebrows drawn into a frown.

"No," he told me. "But it's not natural fog."

Indeed, the temperature dropped by several degrees, and I thought I saw shapes moving through the fog, but it was hard to make out specific details through the air distortion caused by our windy cage. My fur stood on end again, and I remembered the feeling of being watched in the woods behind Crystal's apartment.

"Here's what we'll do," Cindy said. "We'll hold the two wolves in a safe place until Doctor Fortuna gives us the formula and magical secret to curing CLS and Jared signs the company over to me. Then we'll let everyone go, assuming you cooperate."

The teenager I'd seen previously stalked through the fog, and I glanced around, but no one seemed to see her. Indeed, a closer look revealed she stood about three inches off the concrete slab that made the floor of the patio.

"Poor doggies," she said and bent down to look at us.

"Do you see that?" I asked Lonna.

"I do." Her wolf eyebrows, if we could be said to have such things, dropped, and I would have laughed at her almost squint if I hadn't been so afraid.

Something about the girl was eerie and off.

"Who are you?" I asked.

"My name doesn't matter, doggie. The important thing is that there are strange wizards in our territory sapping the energy of the land, and we don't like it."

"Who is 'we'?"

She stood and gestured around. More figures coalesced out of the fog, women in robes and a few men who looked like they came from...

"Oh, gods, you're one of the witches from the seventeenth century. You're a ghost."

"Now that's not very nice. I'm simply not the same kind of alive as you are. But then, you've only half a life in that you haven't embraced your full self." She wagged a finger at me. "Bad doggie, not realizing the gift you've been given with the magic you have."

"It's not a gift if it ruins your life."

She shook her head. "You have no idea what it means to have your life ruined, spoiled doggie. It's selfish of you not to accept all of your parts and live all of your life. You need to learn that lesson."

Well, that was some perspective. True, I'd lost my career and been turned on by my pack, but I still came out of it with my life. It was more than the witches of Salem could say.

The girl continued, "But since you are on our side in this conflict and you were kind to my many times great niece, I will offer you a choice. If you vow to accept your magical side and help others to do the same so that events like those of the past will not happen again, then we will spare the man you love and your friends. If not, we shall drain all of you of your magical energy and destroy you all."

"That's quite the threat." Even as a wolf, I couldn't keep my smartass side from coming out.

Was this what it had come to, that I would have to choose Jared's life over mine? But if it hadn't been for my lycanthropy issues, we wouldn't have reconnected. He might have continued in his fog, and I would have always wondered what had happened to make him not call me. And he would understand my magical restrictions as he learned his own.

It dawned on me that even if the witch-girl hadn't made her threat, I would choose the same. I'd always hate the loss of control, but I'd come to discover a different kind of power and beauty in my wolf. If I didn't have it, I would miss it, especially the heightened senses and the freedom of running through wild places. Plus, I had found someone who really liked all of me including that part, whereas my family hadn't even accepted human me. I'd originally wanted Jared to connect me with a CLS cure, but I realized he had given me a different kind of hope—that I could be fully me.

I couldn't help a tail wag as I said, *"I accept. I will embrace my wolf side."*

"Good doggie." She reached through the swirling wind to pat my head, and the cage disintegrated.

The figures around us grew taller and darker, and I only had time to do one thing—I mentally yelled, *"Run!"*

15

THE NEW NOT-NORMAL

With a blast of something that glowed to my wolf vision, Kurt knocked the confused air elementals over. Jared reached for Cindy, but a wall of fog blocked her, and lightning crackled in what had been a clear sky. The air smelled of ozone, sulfur, and something that tingled in my nose like I'd snorted sparkling water. All my fur stood on end.

"Cindy!" Jared called, but a roaring wind snatched the word from his lips. I wanted him to just leave her, to run, but knowing that he wanted to save his sister in spite of everything she'd done made me admire him even more. My brothers would have already left.

Max and Kurt grabbed Jared and pulled him away from the patio. He continued to look over his shoulder, but he went with them. His agony showed in the tilt of his eyebrows and the set of his jaw. The stupid girl didn't realize what she'd had in a brother who cared for her so much.

Lonna and I darted after them. Merlin seemed to be in conversation with one of the shadowy figures, and after he nodded as though settling something, followed us. The wind blew my fur in different directions, and the entire atmosphere unsettled like it was being ripped apart on the most basic of levels. The thunderclaps grew closer and closer together until they sounded like a tornado, and when I looked back, I saw the strobe light of a lightning storm where we had been. A chorus of screams provided a high-pitched counterpoint to the storm's roar. A howl built in my throat, but I bit it back into a whimper, and Lonna made a similar sound.

No one said anything until we reconvened at Veronica's shop. She sat behind the counter, on which she had arranged different stones. The hum in the air told me she'd been doing magic to strengthen the wizards. She moved from behind the counter and gestured to a couple of robes, and first Lonna and then I changed and put them on. Being human dampened my wolf senses, and I was grateful because every nerve felt raw.

"I don't know what you did to get the angry witches to leave you alone," Merlin told me, "but you're lucky."

"And where were you?" I asked. "Why didn't you do something, and what were you talking about with them?"

He shrugged. "We all have our secrets. I couldn't intervene or I'd get caught. Besides, sometimes people like me need to sit back and let others make the hard choices. I've been punished for interfering before."

"I should have anticipated that they would be awakened with the energy being used," Max told us with a rueful shake of his head. "You can't do that much magic in a place like Salem without attracting attention."

Jared stood by one of the shelves, toying with a purple and green fluorite sphere. "What will happen to them?" he asked. He didn't mean the witches.

Everyone exchanged glances. I honestly didn't know. This was a new world for me, but I could guess it wouldn't be good for Cindy and her crew.

All the hair on my body stood up whenever I thought about

the ghost girl, even now when I stood in human form and tried to ignore how cold the floor was on my bare feet. I couldn't blame the floor for my full-body shiver, though.

Jared pulled me close to him.

"I'm sorry," I said. "I wish I could have saved her."

"So it was you." Merlin approached and looked me over. "You have the makings of an alpha female, you know. You're smart, tough, and have a good sense of when sacrifice is necessary."

I blushed, and Jared asked, "What do you mean?"

"She struck a bargain with the witches," Merlin said. "One of them told me. It's how to get them to leave you alone, of a sort. What did they make you promise, or can you tell us?"

I shrugged. I would tell Jared later, but I didn't want to go into it now. In fact, all I wanted was a nice, warm shower and to crawl into clean sheets.

"Let me take you home," Jared said. He looked pale, his eyes darkened with grief. While I didn't know how to help him deal with his sister's death, I did know a thing or two about sibling rejection or betrayal.

I nodded. "I'd like that so we can at least have a little time together." I tried to close my mouth, but all it did was make me scrunch my face as I stifled a yawn. "Such as it is."

"Take all the time you need." Lonna raised her eyebrows at Max. "You can't take him yet. He still has a lot to do here."

"I'll have to bring his case to the Wizard Tribunal as well as their petition."

"Whoa, what petition?" Jared asked.

"To let the two of you be a mated pair in spite of the fact that the lycanthropes and wizards don't usually like their kinds mixing."

"A what?" I asked. "We've only just reconnected."

Jared put an arm around me. "We'll talk about this later when we're both not so exhausted."

We left, and neither of us said anything on the ride home, although the question—mating, like marriage?—hung in the air between us. When we arrived at my grandmother's house, we found the place clean—no salt rings in the foyer—and a change of sheets on the bed.

"Thank you," I whispered and got no response. I took a quick shower, and when I looked in the mirror after and towel-dried my hair, I saw that someone had drawn a pair of inter-locking hearts in the steam. As far as I knew, no one had been in the bathroom that day but me.

I found Jared downstairs on the couch.

"I don't think I can make it back to Boston," he said. "I'm too exhausted, and my brain can't deal with everything right now."

"Then come upstairs. I think it'll be okay. We can just sleep if you need to."

He grinned and rewarded me with his chocolate chuckle. "Oh, I think it'll be more than that, and I want to do more than sleep with you."

"Oh?"

"I'll race you."

Somehow we both found extra reserves of energy and ran up the stairs. He tackled me to the bed, and I squirmed.

"No fair, you're wearing way too many clothes," I said.

He opened my robe, and I felt the heat of his gaze.

"Gods, you're beautiful."

He slid the robe across me and followed the whisper of silk with his lips. Whenever he found a ticklish spot, I wiggled and made him take something off. And whenever he found a partic-ularly pleasurable place—nipples, curve of my neck, lower—I arched into him and made him pause there. Once he had me panting, I made sure to return the favor and licked and sucked him into submission. Thankfully his dream self was modest, if anything.

"Are you ready?" I asked as I lay across him to get as much skin-on-skin contact as possible.

"Yes, you?"

I answered by sliding down on him, and I closed my eyes with pleasure as he moved beneath me. Keeping a slow pace proved impossible, as he hit all my most sensitive places at once. The orgasm crashed around me with a rumble of thunder, and he gasped his release as well.

"Was that you?" I asked him as we cuddled.

"No, at least I hope not. That could be embarrassing. The neighbors will know every time we do something like this."

I laughed. "They might ask us to if they need their lawns watered."

"And I will always say yes."

"To what?" I held my breath.

"To—what did they say?—being a mated pair with you, or at least exploring the potential benefits of such an arrangement."

I snuggled closer to him. "I like it when you talk business, Mister Steel."

"And I'm always happy when such a lovely opportunity presents itself. Assuming you're amenable to such an arrangement."

"I am," I said. "We can draw up the contract in the morning."

The moonlight coming through the window illuminated his smirk. "I probably don't want to know what your terms will be."

"Just not too many vegetables. We can figure it all out later."

"Thank you," he said. "For everything, but especially for tonight." He relaxed against me, and his even breathing told me sleep overtook him.

I drifted off to sleep in his arms knowing why my grandmother permitted our canoodling and then some—she knew it was meant to be.

$$\sim$$

ON HALLOWEEN, we joined Veronica downtown. Tourists packed the area, of course, and I wondered what the ghostly coven thought about it all. When I asked Veronica, she shrugged.

"They're probably used to it. I would imagine they enjoy it to some degree, as long as we also acknowledge their suffering and how they were punished for being different."

Jared squeezed my hand. "At least you're no longer punishing yourself for that."

"True." I tried not to think about how after the weekend, he would have to return to Boston to meet Kurt and Merlin to start training, although they'd told him they would work with his schedule so he could continue to run his company without Cindy and to come up and see me. I had agreed to help Veronica with the store through the holiday season, and I had finally found my stone. A rose quartz heart similar to the one the teenager had bought now lived on my night-stand as a reminder of both the lessons I'd learned and the promise I'd made to the girl's many times great aunt.

There was no trace of Cindy, Thierry, and the air elementals. I shuddered to think what had become of them. Jared had reported Cindy missing, and the same detective had questioned all of us. Meanwhile, since evidence had pointed to Cindy, Veronica had been cleared, and the authorities assumed Cindy had skipped town.

Only we knew the truth, or what parts of it we could know.

Jared put his arm around me, and we went to stand in line to get into the Salem Witch Experience. It felt so natural and comfortable to be there with him.

Someone touched my arm, and when I looked down, I saw Nona. She gave me a thumbs-up and a wink, and then disappeared.

"What was that?" Jared asked.

"Just further confirmation that this is the right thing, weirdness and all."

"Of course it is. I love you, my little wolf."

"And I love you."

We kissed, and the crowd moved around us. It was one thing to believe in magic; another to embrace it. I knew he would always be there to anchor me, and I would do the same for him. It was our new not-normal, and we were both okay with that.

THANK you for reading A Million Shadows! I hope you enjoyed it. If you wouldn't mind, please consider leaving a review, even a short one, on the site where you bought it or on Goodreads. Reviews are so important for helping books to move higher in the algorithms on book sites, getting the word out, and for helping other readers find books that they'll like or love, too. Thank you so much!

NEXT IN THE LYCANTHROPY FILES UNIVERSE...

If you've enjoyed the Lycanthropy Files *books, you'll love* The Fae Files. *Here's a peek at the first book* **The Shadow Project** ...

The Shadow Project

© *2020 Cecilia Dominic*

Fae Files, Book One

Sometimes even a Fae princess has to agree to an impossible bargain. Unfortunately there's no "fair" in Fae.

Exiled Fae princess Reine has gotten comfortable in the Earth realm, but she'd drop it all in a heartbeat to return home to Faerie. When her scornful mother proposes a pact, Reine knows she better be careful, because Fae bargains are always loaded with tricks...

On the same day she agrees to help smoke out a traitor on a team of scientists, an invisible shifter attacks her in her supposedly ultra-secure home and a teleporting kitten adopts her. She suspects it's all connected, but time is running out for her to figure out how. After discovering a shadowy manipulator is intent on seeing her fail, Reine must confront a deadly conspiracy that reaches into the Fae realm and could spell the end for her kind.

Can Reine unmask a sinister cabal before she loses her ticket home…or her life?

The Shadow Project is the mesmerizing first book in The Fae Files urban fantasy series. If you like snarky heroines, memorable creatures, and thrilling mysteries, then you'll love Cecilia Dominic's spellbinding story.

Buy *The Shadow Project* to pierce the veil today!

You can grab it from your favorite online retailer or ask your local bookstore to order it through Ingram Spark with the ISBN 978-1-945074-59-2

Enjoy the following excerpt from chapter one of The Shadow Project:

The breeze tickled my fingers, and my shoulder cramped from leaning over my desk to the open window, but I didn't move. The little intruder cocked its head, its bandit mask giving it an air of insolence. Just another inch or so and it would pluck the seed from my fingertip. It stretched its neck, and—

The phone rang. In a flurry of wings, the Bohemian waxwing took flight, then alighted on the branch of a nearby shrub and gave me a baleful look.

I checked the number, intending to hit *Ignore* but it was the shop.

"What?"

"I have an emergency." Veronica's voice had an uncharacteristic shrillness.

"What sort of emergency?"

"Something magical. I can't say more. You'll have to see

when you get here." Then she hung up on me. The nerve. But if something had my normally staid clerk in a tizzy, it must be bad.

Still, I couldn't leave the birdie without any help. It had sought me out, but I didn't know why. I placed a thimbleful of seeds in the little dish on my desk just inside the windowsill and said, "Fine, help yourself when I'm gone." Then I grabbed my helmet and ran for my bike.

The trek between my cottage and the village had never seemed so long even with a little Fae enhancement to my motorcycle's speed. I grumbled under my breath the entire way. And here I'd thought everything would calm down now that Veronica had returned from the States, where she'd been caring for her ill sister.

Yet one more reason for me to not depend on anyone unless I absolutely had to. Unfortunately, as the silent financier of the crystal shop in Lycan Village, I had to rely on mortals to take care of things for me. It sucked when they didn't. Hades, I didn't need a crisis right now.

I quieted the roar of the bike as I slid through the back streets and rumbled to a halt behind the shop. I'd managed to keep my involvement a secret – the Lycanthrope Council wouldn't approve if they knew a Fae "interfered" with humans by funding their commerce. They had such a picky definition of what constituted "interference."

Whatever happened must have been bad if she needed me there.

The bell over the back door chimed. I saw she'd turned the sign to "Closed."

"Veronica?" I called softly. My senses were alert for an intruder. Or chaos. Or dark magic. Or any magic at all. The only sensations that I could pick up came from the crystals, each ringing with its own little chime in a chorus of stone bells, a new chime with each of my footsteps.

No, there was something. A whiff of Fae magic, but not strong enough for me to tell where it came from. Something had been here, had gotten past my wards. With my heart in my throat, I walked into the front of the converted cottage to find Veronica holding…a kitten?

"What's the problem?" I asked.

"It's this wee moggie," she said and scratched the creature behind one ear. It angled its head into the caress.

Anger flashed through me and burned out the worry. "You called me here for a *cat*? You said it was something magical."

"It's not just any cat," she said. "There's something seriously wrong with it. Look."

She handed it to me, and I had no choice but to take the warm, soft, purring creature and examine it. The kitten's little face already had character and perhaps the shadow of stripes to come under its lead-colored coat. The most charming part—one white mitten on its front left paw. I checked under the tail—a boy. It fit in the palm of my hand, and I guessed its age to be about six weeks.

"I'm a physician, not a vet," I said. When I ran my hand over it, the silly thing purred louder, but I felt what she must have meant—a frisson of something that didn't feel right.

Still, not an emergency.

I handed the gray kitten back. "He's fine. He just needs some peace and quiet away from his littermates, at least as far as I can tell. Did your time in the States addle your brain, Veronica?"

The little creature looked up at me with big blue eyes that already had flecks of gold and green in them. Ugh. I couldn't resist scratching him under his silky chin. And my fickle frozen heart melted just a touch when he started purring. I mean, who could resist a purring kitten? I might be Fae, but I'm not inhuman.

"Are you sure you wouldn't rather watch him for a day?

Make sure he's all right?" Veronica's Scottish burr made the words sound innocent enough, but I caught the undertone.

"Wait a minute... Is this one of your tricks to get one of your kittens adopted? Again, not an emergency. Besides, he's too young to be away from his mum." I arched an eyebrow and put my hands behind my back so I wouldn't succumb to the temptation to pet the little charmer again.

"No, I'm truly worried for him." With a sigh, she held the kitten to her ample bosom, where he kneaded one of her, er, mounds, his eyes half-closed in bliss. She didn't flinch from his tiny but sharp claws going through her top. Or maybe her sweater was thick enough to handle it.

Then he disappeared.

"What in Hades...?" I asked. To say I was astonished would be an understatement. "Where did he go?"

"Oh, good, he did it. I was afraid he wouldn't and then how could I explain?"

Well, I wasn't going to apologize for snapping at her. "You could've just said that he randomly disappeared." I looked under the cash register counter in her shop but found nothing. "'Acting odd' is a vague way of putting it."

"Would you have believed me?"

"Probably not." Then a slight weight on my shoulder, the sensation of tiny claws digging into my neck, and the sound of a small motor by my left ear told me he'd reappeared. Wherever he'd been, it was cold, and I untangled him from my long hair and held him close to warm him.

"How long has this been going on?"

"For about a week now. Since his ears grew pointed."

"So he's younger than he looks." I held the little lad away from me, and he licked his nose with a tiny pink tongue. Then he licked me, all sweetness and sandpaper. "I truly don't know what to tell you." I didn't often find myself at a loss for words, at least not when dealing with humans, but she had me there.

"So can you please watch him? See what's up? His mother is beside herself and it's taking its toll on the other babies."

She didn't tell me what I already knew—that this would be mama cat's last litter since she'd be spayed once they were all grown and adopted out. But Veronica didn't want any unnecessary deaths on her hands should mama cat breed again on the streets, which could be unkind to animals. I didn't blame her, as much as that sympathy shredded my ruthless Fae reputation. Veronica was the only human I allowed to see this softer side and that was only because she knew what I'd do to her if she revealed my secret. I was a big player in the success of her little shop.

"Fine, I'm intrigued. I suppose I could watch him for a couple of days. What's his name?"

"Raleigh, after Sir Walter Raleigh."

"And you're not afraid he'll come back without his head?"

"Not funny."

I still laughed. "All right, then, Sir Raleigh. Let's get you back to my place and see what's going on with you. Have you noticed any pattern about when it happens?"

She pulled a small spiral-bound notebook from beneath her counter. "I've kept notes. Mostly when he seems to be experiencing some sort of strong feeling. Like just now. But not just positive—it's also happened when he's frightened."

I took the notebook and nodded my approval for her neat, handwritten notes regarding dates and time. "Careful record-keeping, as always."

"Speaking of which..." She rubbed her temples. "I'm still catching up from being gone. Your check will be late."

I should have smote her but it was hard to be in a smiting mood with a purring kitten snuggled on my shoulder. Plus, I knew she'd pay me the rent and my share of the shop's profits when she could. I still couldn't believe the Lycanthrope Council hadn't caught on to our little arrangement. I saw it as an act of rebellion, as did she.

"I know you're good for it. Plus, extra for me figuring out the cat."

"Don't worry, you'll earn that. He's got mischief in his eyes."

The disappearance of the cat from my shoulder confirmed her words, especially when he reappeared on my other shoulder just a minute later. Again, that cold air. And again, I untangled him from my curly, white hair, which he batted at with his little kitten paws. She'd sent me off with plenty of kitten food and instructions, but how could I feed him if I didn't even know where he'd be?

Once I held him in my right hand, I sniffed him. Beyond the delightful smell of cat, there was something else, something familiar, but I couldn't place it. I put him on my chest and zipped up my jacket. He snuggled in and didn't dig in too hard, thankfully.

Yes, in spite of his youth, Sir Raleigh had a certain dignity that deserved the honorific.

When I arrived at my house, my haven in the countryside, I found the door open. I placed Sir Raleigh and his food on top of the mail in the basket to the right of the front door and latched the lid shut. Not that it would deter the cat if he really wanted to escape, but I wouldn't knowingly bring him into harm's way.

With a deep breath, I drew from the energy of the ley line that ran beneath the house, the creek behind it, and the trees over it. Then I wove the nature and ley magic into a web around me that would hopefully capture or deflect any dangerous spells that came my way. Unsophisticated compared to what I could previously do in Faerie, but it was my best for now.

And in case of human intruders, I pulled a small but deadly sharp silver knife from my boot. Its wooden hilt kept the metal from harming me—not that silver did much to me, anyway. Now iron—that was a different matter. I hoped that whoever had intruded upon my home didn't know who or what I was. But who could have found me? I'd kept my address in this realm a secret.

I pushed the door open with the toe of my boot—synthetic, not leather—and crept inside. My eyes adjusted immediately. Nothing seemed amiss, although the air eddied with having recently been disturbed. My spells and wards hadn't been triggered, so who or what could have gotten in?

The Shadow Project is available from most online retailers and can be ordered from any physical bookshop (ISBN 978-1-945074-59-2). Buy The Shadow Project to pierce the veil today!

ABOUT THE AUTHOR

Cecilia Dominic wrote her first story when she was two years old and has always had a much more interesting life inside her head than outside of it. She became a clinical psychologist because she's fascinated by people and their stories, but she couldn't stop writing fiction. The first draft of her dissertation, while not fiction, was still criticized by her major professor for being written in too entertaining a style. She made it through graduate school and got her PhD, started her own practice, and by day, she helps people cure their insomnia without using medication. By night, she writes fiction she hopes will keep her readers turning the pages all night. Yes, she recognizes the conflict of interest between her two careers, so she writes under a pen name. She lives in Atlanta, Georgia, with one husband and two cats, which, she's been told, is a good number of each.

You can find her in the following online places:
Web page: www.ceciliadominic.com
Facebook: www.facebook.com/CeciliaDominicAuthor
Twitter: www.twitter.com/ceciliadominic
Instagram: www.instagram.com/randomoenophile/
Newsletter: http://www.ceciliadominic.com/newsletter

9 781945 074486